SURROUNDED BY

USA TODAY BESTSELLING AUTHOR

MANDY HARBIN

For more information, please join Mandy Harbin's Newsletter!

To all my friends mentioned in previous dedications and to some very important new ones—Rebecca French, Ardyth Neill, Jerry Neill, and fellow author Parker Kincade. Words do not express the appreciation I feel for all you have given me.

PROLOGUE

ARIEL TOSSED her keys onto the entry table made out of reclaimed barn wood before kicking off her shoes and blindly locking the front door behind her. God, she was exhausted. She'd finally formulated that compound and completed the white paper necessary to justify the hundreds of thousands of dollars the local university had been awarded through a federally funded grant. And she'd spent the afternoon explaining the chemical compound and mathematic algorithms necessary to create a biofuel more efficiently with compost.

One man's trash was...well, no need to complete that thought because to her colleagues said trash might become a treasure, but to Ariel it was another project she'd painstakingly nurtured from conception to completion. Just another project that wouldn't get her name in the papers like finding a cure for cancer or discovering the real fountain of youth would. To add insult to cognitive injury, she'd had to deal with vermiculture and microarthropods on this latest assignment. Bugs, *ick*. The compost was a breeding ground for bugs. And she hated bugs.

But Ariel had done what she'd always done—she'd put aside her own feelings for the sake of her job, hoping the next assignment would be the big one. The one that would truly make a name for her, even if just within the scientific community. The one that would allow her to focus on biochemistry and pharmacology, her areas of expertise, rather than general biological and chemical areas.

Ariel strode into the kitchen and grabbed a bottled water from her refrigerator. When she sat down at the tiny bar in the kitchen, she glanced at her notepad. *Krista.* She'd scratched her name down when listening to her messages a couple of weeks ago and hadn't yet called her sister back. Ariel had told herself it was because she was trying to finish up her project at work, but she knew she was lying to herself. Ever since she and Will had gotten divorced a couple of months ago, she'd distanced herself from her family. Not that it had seemed like it to them. Everyone was busy with their own lives, so touching base was usually just a text or a quick email unless it was around the holidays. But she hadn't told anyone about her divorce. Will had filed, so he was the one that had to supply the witness. She'd just signed all the paperwork. Ariel didn't even have to show up at the courthouse. Which was just how she'd wanted it. If she'd been the one to file, she would've had to tell Krista and Krista would've insisted on representing her.

She sighed as she picked up her phone and called her sister.

"Hello?"

"Hey, it's me." As if saying that were necessary.

"How have you been?" Krista asked, but she sounded a little off. Maybe her caseload was still bogging her down.

Ariel told her about her project at work

because that was easier to talk about than what had happened with Will. Krista made little noncommittal noises throughout all the details, evidence of her listening but proof that her mind wanted to be somewhere else. "So are you going to tell me what's bothering you?"

"Um, well, I've just been going through a lot lately. But there was a reason I'd called you before."

"So spill." If Ariel got the focus off herself then maybe she wouldn't feel pressured to talk about Will. But that pressure was mounting, so she knew she'd have to face the music sooner rather than later.

"I met a man."

"Okay, so why did you sound all pitiful when you just said that? Is it because you haven't dated much?"

"Er, no. God, Ariel, I don't know how to even tell you this. It is going to sound crazy. I *know* it is. But you have to believe me because I need your help."

Krista never asked for help. Ever. Ariel's brow furrowed. "What is it?"

"Oh boy," she breathed. "I got assigned to help another attorney with her caseload because she needed to be on location to work on another deal. Her husband's family owns a tree farm in Texas and they were buying some land. Anyway, their property is out in the middle of nowhere. And I mean that. No. Where. So I had to stay with her on the estate."

"Okay," Ariel said when Krista didn't continue right away.

"Do you believe in the paranormal?"

Huh? "Do you mean ghosts or something like that?"

"Something like that."

"Um, I believe that if it can't be scientifically proven then it doesn't exist. You know that."

"Oh, there's no doubt they exist," Krista mumbled.

"Who? Just spit it out already."

"I need your word you will not breathe a word of this to anybody."

"Even to your new shrink I need to put on speed dial after this conversation?" She took a drink of her water and sat it down as she smiled.

"I'm being serious, Ariel."

"Yes, okay. You have my word."

"I became involved with one of the family members on that estate and accidentally learned a major family secret."

Ariel sat up a little straighter, but kept quiet this time when Krista paused.

"They turn into mountain lions. All of them. They shift into animals," Krista whispered that last part.

"Like werewolves?" So the psychiatrist's comment wasn't really a joke. Had Krista been working so hard that her cheese had finally slipped off her cracker? "They don't exist, honey."

"Don't patronize me, Ariel! I wouldn't be telling you if I didn't need your help and because I need said help, you'll get to witness it firsthand."

"Well, I'm sorry, but you're right. This is crazy."

"Just hear me out. The thing is, this family has a feral need to mate with any available female. When I got the assignment to work on the property, I had to pretend I was involved with a man. That's how dangerous this is. It's deadly. They can only be around attached females, even their sexual encounters. Seriously, Toby had a brother that died because a woman he was screwing announced she was now divorced, so he forced a mating. They fought to the death because a female lion taken against her will attacks the male and there is no bond of love to keep the male from fighting back."

"And Toby is...?"

"The family member I became involved with."

"Did you sleep with him?" Ariel had to find out where this was coming from. Maybe Krista had had a bad breakup and was now delusional.

"Yes."

"Did he mate with you?"

"No," her voice cracked. Seemed like Ariel was on the right track with the bad breakup idea.

"Are you in love with him?"

"Yes, which is why I need your help. I need you to work your chemical magic and figure out some drug that could suppress their feral need to mate with just any available woman."

"So you think if you fix them that this Toby man would want you back? Is that it?"

"No! I'm not doing this for me. I'm

doing this for them. All of them. They are stuck there. Isolated on that acreage. I want to give them the freedom that we all take for granted."

"So you really believe they turn into animals?"

"Yes. I saw it with my own eyes. They need help. You have the knowledge that might give them what they need. You're my sister and know how important this family is to me, so I know you'd not only be professional about it but keep this matter private. And you're married, so I know that won't be an issue with the guys."

At the mention of Ariel's failed marriage, guilt washed over her. She should tell Krista. Right now. It'd get her out of this crazy plan and maybe then she could focus on helping Krista heal from her breakup.

"Please. Just come see for yourself," Krista pleaded softly.

And what if this were all true like her sister believed? Ariel could finally work on something that'd actually be in the concentration areas she'd studied in college. It wouldn't hurt to check it out. Her project was finalized at work and she had some time off anyway.

And a discovery like this could make her career. Because if it were true, no way was she keeping a lid on this.

"I'm in."

CHAPTER ONE

"Fuck!" Rob yelled and jumped to his left as a limb came crashing toward him. He needed to get his head out of his ass and back on his job. It wasn't like he was some paper-pushing pansy. He couldn't afford to be distracted.

But the truth was he'd been nothing but distracted since Krista twitched her rear back into his brother's life a couple of days ago. Since then, Toby had been M.I.A., leaving all the work to Rob and his brothers. Not that Rob could fault him. Hell, he'd stay in bed for weeks if he had a mate too. But that really wasn't what had been distracting him. It was the fact that Krista had brought the knowledge, had brought *hope* back with her. She'd said her sister might have some answers that'd get them out of the prison of this land, and it was that hope that had his brain twisted tighter than rope. He really did love it here, but he often wondered if that was just because this was all he really knew. Well, he loved the serenity, not the isolation. Not the limitations. If he were free of the struggles of his beast, Rob felt as if he'd be able to fully embrace his life—all of his life—for the first time. Because he'd once and for all be able to find a mate to live out his years with. Hope. He was almost too scared to embrace it. Although his brothers had achieved the dream without any medical or chemical intervention, Rob wasn't stupid enough to look a gift horse in the mouth. If Mini-Krista could come up with some voodoo magic that'd turn his deepest desires into a reality, then he was all for it.

"You okay, bro?" Jack yelled from atop the ridge. Rob just waved his arm, signaling his response, then dropped both hands to his knees as he sucked in a lungful of air.

Exhaling, he straightened and wiped the sweat from his brow. "Lunch time yet?" he called out to Jack.

"'Bout that time. Toby just texted me

that Krista's sister is on her way. Should be here within thirty."

That'd give them just enough time to get up to the main house and eat before meeting the chick with the answers. God, he hoped she could do something for them. Rob grabbed his gear so he wouldn't have to make the trip back to this section after lunch. He'd be working on the other side of the ridge with Josh this afternoon, assuming he'd even be able to do a better job of concentrating then.

With a new female on the property, he highly doubted that, because if she looked anything like her sister, Rob knew getting help with his beast wasn't going to be the only thing dominating his mind.

———

"THEY'RE HERE," Jack muttered as he looked out the window. Could he sound any more brutish? Lord, Rob had no idea what any woman could see in his brother. Sure he had the same physical traits as the rest of them, tall, dark hair, light eyes—though Jack's were blue—but his brother could be...well, a dick, actually. Where

Rob was the jokester around here, Jack was the polar opposite. He was hard as nails when it came to work or anything else. He tried taking charge as if he were the oldest and ordering Rob and his brothers around whenever he got the chance. Jack wasn't the boss. He was a jerk. "She's not as lush as Krista, but she'll do."

"*She'll do?*" Rob hissed. "What the fuck, Jack?"

"Jackson! That's no way to act toward our guest. She's here to help. And she's a married woman. You will respect the bond she has with her husband." Their father, Thomas, was never one to tolerate bad behavior and Rob breathed a sigh of relief.

"What's going on?" Josh asked as he and Mikaela entered hand-in-hand. "Krista and Toby are on their way up with her sister. I could hear you in the hall. Now's not the time to be bickering."

"Jack is being a dick," Rob said, throwing an evil glance in his jackass of a brother's direction.

"Fuck off, Rob. Don't even pretend you don't want a piece of her ass. You're just being quiet and noble in hopes it'll pay off.

At least I'm man enough to admit what I want."

"Enough!" At Thomas' tone, the room quieted and it was a good thing because Rob could hear footsteps outside and rumblings of muted voices.

The door swung open and Rob had to keep his jaw from hitting the floor. Mini-Krista was a vision. Beautiful. As she walked in, he took stock of her, drinking in every detail. Her lovely hair, big eyes, tiny nose. But as he cataloged everything from her hair to her baggy clothes, he realized the little nickname he'd given her in passing actually fit. Krista wasn't fat. Not at all, but her sister was thin. Almost too thin. Did she not ever eat? She didn't look sickly, but Rob had to tamp down this almost sudden, overwhelming concern for her that consumed him out of nowhere. What the fuck? She was a married woman. He looked away, needing to take his eyes off her to set his thoughts straight. It was probably Jack's behavior earlier that made him have that reaction. As he glanced around the room, his eyes lit on his father before landing on Jack. Rob had to stifle a growl. Jack had the look of a predator tracking its next meal and readying him-self to strike at the first moment of weakness.

"This is Thomas Woods, Toby's fa-ther," Krista said as his dad stepped up to her. He took her hand and shook it once before dropping it.

"It's a pleasure, Mrs. Yates."

"Oh no, you don't. It's Ariel, and don't you forget it, Thomas."

God, her voice. So angelic. But if she were an angel, she had to be a fallen angel sent here to tempt him. Because he couldn't have her and he knew without a shadow of a doubt that her being here was going to be the greatest test of his will.

His dad smiled at her. "I think I'm going to like having you here."

That made one of them.

Krista turned to her side. "This is Toby's brother, Josh, and his mate, Mikaela."

"Nice to meet you two." What was it about her voice? Did she drink from ambrosia?

"And these two over here are Jack and Rob, Toby's other brothers."

Jack stepped forward at the first mention of his name and shook her hand. Bastard.

He lingered.

"*Jack,*" their father reproached silently. Rob was thankful Thomas had utilized their ability to speak telepathically to call his brother out. Jack let go of her hand and stepped back.

Rob moved forward, gently taking her hand. Not as soft as he'd imagined, but not as calloused as his. She looked up at him with those big, round eyes and he just melted. He got the sense that she thought she was a tough woman, but that it was also a ruse. Her tongue slipped out, wetting her lips, just before her mouth quirked into the tiniest of smiles. Not knowing how to respond to that, Rob nodded at her briefly before dropping her hand and taking a step back.

"So, Mrs., er...Ariel, what are your plans and when do you want to get started?"

"Well, I want to start right now." She shrugged as if she did this sort of thing all the time and doing her voodoo magic was no big deal. She looked at Jack before looking at Rob again. He held her gaze, trying not to think beyond anything but what she could do for him. *Oh, the things she could do for me. I could take her to bed and not let her leave for...stop it!* "I think there's been a misunderstanding. I'm not married anymore. How does that make you feel?"

The air left his lungs and the ringing in his ears might've been mental shouting from his family, but Rob couldn't focus. Couldn't function. She wasn't taken. She was an available woman.

"What the hell are you talking about, Ariel Michelle? What about Will?"

Will? Her husband? She was married. Why did she just say she wasn't anymore? Rob's body was shaking. The need to shift and claim was scratching at the surface. Was this part of the work she needed to do? Krista would know if her own sister had gotten a divorce. This possibility bought him time, but only the barest amount.

"We grew out of love a long time ago and got tired of the pretense. Our divorce was final three months ago."

Fuck, now she was looking directly at Rob and Jack, and Rob didn't know if he was more pissed at what she was saying or the fact that she was even looking at Jack. His brother would be keeping his mangy paws off her!

"I'm not involved with anyone either. I'm a totally and completely available woman. How does that make you feel?"

Her eyebrow quirked up and Rob had to restrain himself as his feet started to move toward her. The mantra, *"Mine,"* kept chanting in his head, but at the moment he wasn't entirely sure if it was his internal monologue or Jack staking his claim.

"Shit, Ariel, are you lying?" Krista squeaked as she grabbed her sister's arm.

"My divorce papers are in my briefcase. You can call Will if you want. He's vacationing in Italy with his new girlfriend, though."

Jack growled, and Rob turned his head, hissing at his brother. *"Mine!"* This time, Rob made sure all his family knew he was claiming her. Fuck his brother. *"You'll have to go through me, Jack."*

"Fine by me, little kitten. I'll fucking eat you for dinner before I claim my new mate."

"Fuck, get her out of here!" Josh yelled

right as Rob and Jack shifted into snarling mountain lions.

Rob growled and lunged for Jack. Jack bit into Rob's neck as they rolled over, snapping, hissing, and scratching at each other.

"Boys!" Thomas yelled, but it barely registered. As soon as Rob would get the upper hand, Jack would best him, tipping the odds back in his brother's favor. Jack might be older, but they were pretty equally matched. The only way one would actually win would be if the other were dead because neither would tuck tail and run.

Jack was knocked off Rob, but before Rob could attack again, Josh was on him, pinning him down. Rob hissed at Josh in his lion form and turned to look for Jack. This wasn't Josh's fight. What he'd found was that Toby had also shifted and had Jack cornered.

"*She's gone,*" Jack announced as he stared down at Rob. "*The girls got her out.*"

Rob roared.

"*I know, man, but fight it. This isn't you.*"

"*I'm a damn animal. Of course it's me. It's all of us!*"

"But you don't want to hurt her. And I can't let you. I won't let you."

Rob hissed because he knew deep down that Josh was right. Rob looked at Jack. He was still pacing as if he were caged.

"He's wound up, too. That's Toby's mate's sister. Krista is freaking out and Toby will not allow anything to upset his mate. I'm warning you, get control now... otherwise, Toby will rip you a new one. He's already ready to kill Jack with all the mental screaming and demanding he's been doing."

Rob had been so caught up in his own desire, his own need to claim her that he hadn't paid much attention to Jack. With how possessive Jack was by nature and how he'd acted just by seeing her outside before even meeting her, Rob really shouldn't be surprised by Jack's response.

He shifted and Josh followed.

"Fine. She's not around. I'm in control. But you have to know how much I want her."

"That's your animal talking. You don't even know her." Josh moved and offered his hand to help Rob up.

"Like you knew Mikaela?" Rob challenged once he was standing.

"Mikaela's different. I knew that the moment I first smelled her."

Rob also knew there was something different about Ariel, but he didn't have to explain that to his brother. There was only one thing Josh needed to understand. "She's mine."

Josh sighed, putting his hands on his bare hips. "You can't decide that for her. She has to leave."

"No way!" Rob stepped up, ready to battle again. His testosterone, adrenaline, and feline all demanded it. They were not taking her away from him.

Josh's hands flew up in a surrendering gesture. "Think about it, Rob. She's not safe here. We can talk to her—as in me and Toby and the girls—and see if there's a way for her to do her research or whatever she needs to do from another location. We can try to work around this and still get her help." Rob shook his head, but before he could voice his rejection, Josh continued. "Think about why she's really here. If she can come up with a way to set you free, then you can have your pick of any available woman. Without taking her by force."

Rob stared. He knew his brother was being logical.

He didn't care.

Once he'd set his eyes on Ariel, he knew she was the one for him. He'd never, *never*, had that kind of reaction toward a woman before. He hadn't known she was available when he'd first seen her either. For him, that left no doubt.

"You're right." Rob still needed Ariel around to do her work. If their father decided it was too dangerous, he might axe the whole idea and Rob would never have the chance to see her again. At least if he went along with the plan, he could figure something out. He glanced at Jack. He'd shifted back, but Toby was in his face, whispering heatedly, stabbing his finger into Jack's chest.

Jack's eyes met his over Toby's shoulder. The challenge in them almost sent him back into an animalistic rage.

Ariel belonged to Rob. Period. And he'd make sure Jack understood that. And Ariel, too.

In time.

CHAPTER TWO

"Have you lost your freaking mind?"

Ariel watched as her sister paced manically in the bedroom, waiting for her to calm down and be rational. Ariel had to see what she was working with. Hearing a story about mountain lion shifters was totally different that witnessing the phenomena first hand.

"No, but I'm glad to see you haven't lost yours. I'd had every intention of making you an appointment with a doctor after I'd come out here. I seriously thought you were nuts." Well, there was a part of her that had been salivating at the possibility Krista was telling her the truth.

Her sister whirled. "So you thought

tempting their beast was the best plan of attack?" she asked incredulously.

"Quickest."

"You're unbelievable! And what about Will? Did you ever plan on telling me that little bit of info? Who handled your divorce? Oh my God, Ariel, he could've taken you to the cleaners."

"Dial back the legal crap, Krista. I might not be an attorney, but I can damn well read a decree and decide if it's fair. We split everything and have no children. Easy cheesy."

"But you two were so in love."

"I don't believe in love anymore. It was foolish to ever believe in it in the first place. It's a chemical process involving things like oxytocin, dopamine, serotonin, vasopressin, norepinephrine, testosterone, estrogen, I can go on and on." Ariel waved her hand dismissively.

"Mikaela cleared her throat. "Even though I agree with Krista on the divorce issue, I think we need to stay on track here. You've put yourself in a seriously dangerous situation and we need to get you out of here."

"I'm not going anywhere," Ariel said,

sitting on the big bed in the middle of the room.

"The hell you're not, Ariel Michelle. You cannot stay here if you're not taken."

"And just how did you manage to be at this estate in the first place? I don't remember *you* being in any relationship recently."

"Umm—"

"I needed her help with my caseload while the Woods purchased the adjoining land. We told the men she was in a relationship when she came out here."

"And they believed you? Just like that?" she asked as she grabbed her iPad from her big purse. "Fascinating," she mumbled, typing some notes. This brought the honor system to a whole new level.

"Yes, well, we could've told them the same thing about you had we known you weren't married anymore. But that option is moot now. If we go back and tell them it was a test, part of your research, they'll demand proof. Divorce records are public and we *do* have Internet here. I'm pretty sure both of the guys are researching you now as we speak."

"I don't want the pretense. I need them

to know the truth. I need to understand everything if I am going to be able to help. I can't formulate a medication to address an issue if I don't honestly comprehend what that issue really is." Why didn't they understand? It wasn't like she was testing something on lab rats to verify any side effects to chemicals. They wanted her to essentially treat these men for a condition that was undocumented. Hell, she wasn't a doctor.

Mikaela sat next to her on the bed. "So what do you propose?"

"She's leaving!" Had Krista just stomped her foot like she used to do when she was a toddler?

"Let's be rational here, Krista. We need to at least know what's going on in that little head of hers before we can make any decisions here." She turned to Ariel. "But if Thomas wants you gone, we're going to have our work cut out for us. That's why I need you to explain to me what your game plan is. If I think it's worth a shot, I can try to reason with him."

Her sister was still fuming, so Ariel figured she needed the Mikaela chick on her side. But there was part of the plan that made even her nervous. She'd have to put on her big girl panties and follow through with it. If she wanted to make a name for herself in her career, she had to.

"I've been working on an aggression compound. Actually, the university has been working on a product for years, so I'm just tweaking the formula to ensure it's safe enough for human consumption. I just need to mix the chemicals based on their height and weight and start administering it to them. But I think in order for me to make sure it works under all circumstances, I need one of them to volunteer to be my test subject."

"Why do you need a test subject if you're going to medicate them both?" Krista asked, her arms crossed.

"Because if this is going to be a long term treatment, I need to know when and how it is best administered. Once a day? Three times a day? Once a week? Large dose once a month with smaller doses throughout? There are too many questions and I need to test the limit of the drugs to ensure their effectiveness.

"Test the limit the drug?" Mikaela asked. "What exactly do you mean by that?"

Here goes nothing...

"Just the way it sounds." When Krista gasped, Ariel knew comprehension was dawning. "I'm going to tease the hell out of whoever volunteers."

———

ROB SAT IN HIS ROOM, locked in like a damn wild animal, and logged onto his Skype account. This was re-fucking-diculous. His father had called a meeting to discuss Ariel, and he wasn't allowed anywhere near her.

But neither was Jack. Rob took solace in that. Very little solace.

When he'd laid eyes on Ariel today, his insides burned. He'd felt a connection to her that he'd never felt before. It wasn't rational. But neither was turning into a feline. Nothing was rational in his life, so why did he expect seeing his mate for the first time would be anything short of powerful? He knew both Josh and Toby had felt something different, something miraculously overpowering with their mates early on. Maybe this was just how it was for them.

Once a mate was identified, that was it. It was her or no one else.

God, he was being insane. He hardly knew this woman. If he didn't chill out, he'd scare her away. At least Jack was naturally brooding. This newly developed situation probably had him clawing at the walls to get out and get to her, which would only make Rob look that much better.

He growled low in his throat. He wouldn't let Jack touch her. She belonged to Rob. End of fucking story.

The call came through and he accepted it. He had to grab the chair he was planted in to keep from touching the monitor like a love-struck fool and stroking Ariel's beautiful face. She was definitely too skinny, but her beauty would always outshine no matter her weight.

"I demand to be released at once, Dad. This is highly uncalled for," Jack commented from his connection.

"Calm down. I've talked things over with the ladies and have a better understanding of the course Ariel would like to take. I must say I'm not entirely pleased with what has happened or with this methodology she'd like to implement. I feel that since you two will be the ones involved, you both need to understand what will be happening. Then you can make a decision on whether she stays or goes."

Ariel's eyes grew wider for only a second before cutting to Thomas and then looking straight ahead again. If Rob had to guess, she didn't look very pleased with this. If his waiflike angel wanted to stay, by God, she would. He'd do whatever necessary to ensure it.

And he wasn't stupid enough to pretend he wasn't being selfish with that noble thought.

His father looked at Rob, then Jack, and proceeded to tell them and the rest gathered in the den on the other end of the monitor just what medications she planned on trying on them. One shot a day to start out. Testing aggression. Possibly more medication. So far, nothing seemed too horrible. Rob knew this wasn't going to be a cakewalk.

"Just what kind of testing do you expect us to do? Torture us? Keep us locked up in our rooms? Or worse, in chains? Sorry, honey, you're hot and all, but no way. I say give us the medication and observe us," Jack said, arms crossed over his chest, eyes narrowed. Then he half-smiled. "Unless you want to observe me privately."

"Jackson!"

"What, Dad? Those are honest questions." Then he looked at Ariel. "And an honest offer." He wasn't smiling this time. Just being the dick he always was.

"It doesn't matter to me. I say she can do whatever she wants. She's the professional here," Rob said, tamping down his need to vocalize just what he wanted from her. He gave her what he hoped was a soft smile, and the startled smile she gave him in return made his dick twitch. Such a beauty.

"Rob?" she asked, looking toward him. His heart raced. The sound of his name on her lips did some very naughty things to his body. He wanted to hear her moan it the next time his name slipped passed her lips.

"Yes, angel?"

That smile. He couldn't help but return the warm gesture.

"Would you be willing to help me do some testing? I only need to test one of you."

"Wait just a damn minute! No way in hell am I staying in this room while Rob gets poked with needles. He's just trying to poke her back," Jack barked.

Rob's head snapped in his brother's direction, a growl ripping from his throat before he could even stop it. He was going to shred his brother to pieces!

"Enough, boys!" Thomas said, then turned to Ariel. "Sweetheart, I'm aware of your plan, but I'm not sure if this is smart. I have to say I think it's very dangerous. Just look at them. They are too primal and they are not even in the same room with you.

Shit. Rob had to get control of himself. Otherwise, he'd lose his opportunity before it even started. He took a deep breath, facing his father. "Dad, if we don't do something now, we may never get another shot."

"I'll do it," Jack said with an heir of righteousness. "I'm older. It's. My. Fucking. Turn."

Their father sighed. "Jack, regardless of which one of you she tests, both of you will be getting the medication," Thomas said. Then he turned to Ariel. "I think this has to be your call."

Her cheeks flushed a satiny pink, and Rob's head cocked to the side as if his cat were trying to gauge it. Then her gaze landed on him.

"Will you help me, Rob? I promise not to make it too painful for you."

She picked me. Rob felt his whole body heat, warmth rushing through him. But the sweet feeling that accompanied his mate's initial trust in him quickly turned into an almost overpowering urge to roar in victory.

And a crippling need to take her right now.

How was he going to be able to be near her and not force her to mate with him? His animal didn't care. It only saw a relief to its primal heat. But Rob knew she was taking a big step by asking him. She was relying on him to do this for her. He could not let her down. He wouldn't.

"It'd be my pleasure, angel."

CHAPTER THREE

"You don't have to do this," Krista pleaded with her sister. "I know you eat, live, breathe your job, but this is going way above the call of duty."

Ignoring her, Ariel handed over the syringe containing Jack's initial dosage. "Swab the area with an alcohol pad first. On his hip. Then uncap the needle, tap it a few times like this," she flicked the syringe as a demonstration. "Gently push the plunger until the air is extracted, then you're ready."

"You're really going to go through with this, aren't you?"

Ariel took a calming breath and squared her shoulders. It wouldn't do to get into a fight with her sister, but they'd been over this and over this. "Thomas said they will not leave me alone with Rob until they are sure he is under control. I have no desire to be raped and killed. I value the work I do. I think I can help. And *you* asked me to in the first place. Please just let me do my job."

"They are feral, Ariel. You got a glimpse of it earlier today. You have no idea the need they have to bond with a mate. It's all encompassing. I know I asked for your help. I want them free of the chains that bind them to this land, but I don't want you to get hurt. When I asked for your help, I didn't mean I wanted you to seduce one of them!"

"I am conducting tests. Not hooking up."

"There's a term for a woman who uses her body in the name of *work*."

Ariel walked over and grabbed her bag of goodies. Tools she'd gotten at the adult store in St. Louis before coming out here. Krista had just likened her to a prostitute and it was hard for her to deny the allegation with tricks of the trade in her hand. "I'm doing it and that's final. You'll thank me later. They all will." Her heart pounded as guilt prickled. They wouldn't thank her if she exposed them in the name of her real work.

Krista walked over to her and hugged her. "Be careful."

Ariel released her and rubbed her arm reassuringly. "I'll be fine. Thomas has me staying in this cabin next to Rob's. Jack has been instructed to stay in the house and work on the south side of the property. He and I won't cross paths. His medication will be administered by Thomas's right-hand man, Jeffery, and Thomas will observe him for any side effects. As for Rob, let me handle that, okay?"

A knock sounded on the door, allowing butterflies to swarm erratically in Ariel's belly for the first time since coming back to the cabin.

"It's Mikaela. They're ready," she announced through the door.

"Fine," Krista whispered heatedly. "You win. I'll let you handle Rob, but you damn well better tell me if anything goes wrong."

"Deal." Ariel grabbed her bag and opened the door. "I'm ready."

Mikaela looked at her with a mixture of

worry and admiration, and that little bit of guilt from earlier came back. Ariel tamped it down. She didn't have time to worry about that right now.

"I'm coming too," Krista said.

Mikaela chuckled. "Girl, your man has been on the warpath since your sister here made that little announcement about not being a taken woman. First, he practically beat Jack into submission, then after the meeting, he gave Jack another round of, um, brotherly encouragement to behave."

"I can only imagine what kind of encouragement Toby provided." Krista grinned.

Mikaela turned to Ariel. "And he's been reading Rob his rights in Rob's cabin ever since. We all view you as family since you're Krista's sister, but you're his *mate's* sister, so he feels an even stronger obligation to protect you. And he will. Especially since he knows how worried Krista is about all this. If I know Toby, he's probably fighting every primal instinct to lock you up just to keep his mate from being upset."

"Good," Krista said.

"Don't give her any ideas," Ariel groaned.

Mikaela stepped aside and the girls followed her to the cabin next door. This estate was really very refreshing—rustic but not jarringly so. Ariel didn't like the camo motif. She understood its need for function, but why anybody decorated in the stuff, she'd never understand.

When Krista opened the door and they stepped into Rob's cabin, Ariel kept her expression even...with great difficulty. Rob was shirtless and bound to a wooden chair. His worn jeans hung low and showed how cut he actually was. His legs were tied to the chair too. God, his bare feet even looked sexy. But the hottest thing about him was his gaze. The way his eyes peered into her. Like they were already alone and he was ready to pounce.

Rob growled, showing fangs, and she gasped. She didn't know they had fangs like that unless they'd already shifted. Maybe she should've gotten some additional information from Krista and Mikaela before walking into the lion's den. Literally.

"Come," Rob rasped. "Now." His arms flexed within their bindings and Ariel went rigid, wondering if they'd hold.

Toby growled next to him, his eyes focused solely on his brother.

"We should get started," Josh said.

"I have the medication right here." Ariel started to step forward, but Josh threw his hand up, stopping her progression, and moved toward her, blocking her view from Rob.

And apparently Rob didn't like that because a blood-curdling roar came from his direction.

Krista squeaked and jumped next to her at the same time Josh stepped to the side, allowing Rob to see his fill. Toby's head snapped in Krista's direction at her distress, then whipped toward Rob. He crouched in front of his brother, a menacing growl slipping past his lips. Ariel shivered. For some reason, the softer growl from Toby sounded more deadly and a hell of a lot more terrifying than the loud roar Rob made.

Rob hissed at Toby and wiggled in his chair, struggling to get free.

Josh stepped up and took the syringe from Ariel. "I'll do it. You stay here."

When Ariel starting giving Josh the instructions, Rob's gaze flew to her and he snarled. She quickly finished the steps Josh needed to administer the medication and watched as he approached Rob from the side, making sure to not to block his view of Ariel.

She watched as Josh bent in front of Rob and blindly handed the needle over to Toby. When Josh grabbed the waistband of Rob's jeans, Ariel swallowed. There was no turning back now. She watched in rapt fascination as Josh unfastened Rob's jeans and slowly slid the zipper down so he could get to the injection site.

"Damn," Ariel breathed when Rob's rock hard erection sprang free. He was freaking huge!

Rob had been making low growls and hisses at his brother as he worked the closure on his jeans, but when Ariel spoke, his attention snapped back to her. His growl got softer, broken. What's that... *Is he purring?*

"I think he likes that you find his, um, member impressive," Krista whispered.

Toby looked at Krista and growled. "You shouldn't be looking. You only look at me."

Ariel watched as her sister fought a

smile. But she turned to the side, giving her back to them. "Better, sweetie?"

His next growl sounded more like a groan. "I love your ass."

She wiggled it and the animalistic sound got louder, playful.

"Chill, you two," Mikaela said, then turned to Ariel. "Just like a couple of newlyweds." She shook her head but smiled. "I think that's good, Josh."

"Okay, kitten. I want you and the other ladies to stay over there until we're sure he won't break free and the drugs are working." Josh lifted his arm, needle poised for entry.

"Wait!" Ariel shrieked and quickly stepped forward. She needed to gather as much data as she could. "Can you tell me how you feel?" she asked Rob softly.

"Why don't you grab my dick and tell me how I feel?"

"No."

Rob roared. "That wasn't a request. You will submit to me. You are *mine*."

Without warning, Josh stabbed the needle into Rob's hip. Rob yelped and hissed at his brother.

Ariel watched him as he struggled in

his chair, trying to break free, growling and hissing at everyone, at no one.

Then minutes later, his movements eased, his head falling back as he gasped in air, sweat trickling down his temple. No one moved for what seemed like an eternity. Ariel just watched. Waited.

Rob slowly moved his head, his eyes seeking her. She held her breath as he found her, eager to hear him now that he'd received his first dose.

"I think I'm okay."

"Do you feel like you need to mate with her?" Josh asked.

Rob frowned. "I believe I have control of myself. My lion."

Ariel stepped closer and Toby tensed beside Rob.

"Can you tell me how you feel now?"

Rob chuckled. "I guess I can't give you the same answer as before, huh?"

Ariel laughed nervously. He seemed relaxed. He wasn't growling or hissing or fighting his restraints. She quickly scanned his body. *Mostly relaxed.* His penis was still fully erect. She turned to Josh. "Take his vital signs. Let's make sure he's not about to have a heart attack before I continue." She dug into her bag, pulling out a swab kit. "And here, take this and swab the inside of his cheek while you're at it."

Josh worked quickly as Ariel watched. The three brothers seemed to be staring at each other intently. Then she saw an infinitesimal shake of Rob's head.

"They're speaking telepathically."

Ariel nodded. A few weeks ago she had been knee-deep in compost and now she was about to be on her knees...um, yeah. She knew. Her nerves were back in full force now that Rob seemed to be doing well under the medication.

"This is amazing!" Josh said as he clapped Rob on the back. "You seem healthy as a horse. I can't believe you're not trying to fight to get to her anymore."

"Let's not do a victory dance yet," Ariel warned. "This is all part of the process."

"Right, of course," Josh said, grinning. He looked at Rob and chuckled. Then he looked at his mate. "I think we can go."

"C'mon, Krista," Mikaela said. "We need to get Jack medicated, too."

Toby watched Rob, eyes narrowing. "You're sure you're in control? If you hurt one hair on her head, I will make you bleed. Understood?"

Rob nodded.

Toby straightened and walked toward Krista. "I can stay. Whatever she's going to do, I can watch from the other side of the room to make sure he doesn't do anything to hurt her. She's very tiny and he's incredibly strong."

Ariel's face got really hot all of a sudden. No way in hell did she want a witness to this next part. She glanced at Rob, trying to think of something quickly to say that'd keep her from having an audience.

Rob's head cocked to the side as he watched her. Without looking away, he said, "That won't be necessary, bro."

Toby made a frustrated sound at the back of his throat, his eyes on his mate. "It's your call, baby."

Krista looked at Ariel. Ariel hoped the pleading in her eyes was working.

"Let's go, sweetie, and leave her to her work."

Ariel sighed, relieved.

Toby's shoulders relaxed as he wound his arm around his mate. "Okay."

"You will let us know the minute you

need something, anything. Right?" Krista gave Ariel a stern look, and Ariel nodded.

"Good luck," Mikaela said, a small smile playing at her lips as she and Josh left. Krista and Toby left right behind them. Her sister looked one last time over her shoulder before shutting the door.

Ariel was now alone with Rob. The relieved feeling from moments ago was now gone. There really was no backing out. The compound had worked. She'd seen it with her own eyes. He was virile and determined to have her one minute then lucid and calm the next. Still sexy has hell, though. God, she needed to let that thought go. Rob was hot, no doubt about that, but she was here to do a job. A job she was beginning to wonder if she could keep herself detached from in order to complete.

Just do it.

She walked toward Rob. He watched her. Eyes not animalistic. Teeth not fangs. Just watched like someone who was curious about what movie was showing at the theater. But as she got closer, she noticed the muscles in his forearms corded. There seemed to be more lurking behind the surface than his calm curiosity.

"Um, okay." Her voice cracked, so she took a steadying breath. "This is a bit unorthodox—"

"Compared to what? The family of werewolves who live in Dallas?" Ariel gasped and he chuckled. "Kidding, angel."

She laughed nervously, realizing that part of her nerves was due to how attractive this man was. This would be so much easier if he were hideous, like a mangy old alley cat, missing an eye and covered in bald patches.

"Right, well, unorthodox is subjective in this sense." She took a few steps closer. Now he had to tilt his head up to look at her. "What I mean is the way I'm going to test the effectiveness of this drug and your endurance to it isn't what I'd call standard protocol."

"I'll do whatever you want."

Ariel cleared her throat and shifted her weight to her other leg, stalling. *Here goes nothing.* She stepped right up into his personal space. "Do you find me attractive?"

A small growl rumbled in his chest, but he didn't let it out. "Incredibly. You're the sexiest woman I've ever seen and, animal or not, I would love nothing more than to be buried deep inside you."

Good. If only his animal side wanted her, then she wasn't sure how well this testing method would work. She smiled at him, her tongue slipping out to wet her lips. Rob watched as she traced her upper lip, and he moaned softly.

"I'm going to tease you, Rob. You'll be surrounded by temptation greater than any you've ever experienced. I'm going to drive you so insane with want that you'll be begging me for it."

CHAPTER FOUR

Rob stared at the vixen before him and wanted to scream in victory, wanted to take her in his arms, wanted to shout her name as he fucked her all night long. His dick grew painfully hard. He wanted her right now. Needed her with an ache he couldn't identify because it wasn't a feeling he'd ever experienced before in his life.

Because she's my mate.

"I need you to tell me if I cross the line and do anything that makes you uncomfortable, but I need you to be able to tell the difference between a comfort issue due to morality or a comfort issue because the medication isn't working as effectively as it should. Do you think you can tell the difference between the two?"

He nodded because if he opened his mouth, he wasn't sure if he'd order her to start. He felt in control of his lion, but that didn't mean his nature wouldn't kick in.

"I'm going to leave you bound for now. As the testing progresses, we will gradually allow you more liberties."

When he didn't respond, she took the last remaining step up to him, her legs brushing his. He watched her closely. Her breathing was slightly erratic and her hands trembled. She gripped the tops of his shoulders, her heat searing his bare skin. When she lifted her leg and threw it over his lap, straddling him, he caught a faint scent of her arousal.

"Oh fuck," he groaned, squeezing his eyes shut as she seated herself fully across him, his cock blanketed by the warm apex of her thighs.

"This okay?" she asked a little breathless.

He jerked his head in a nod, trying to maintain control for her but wishing like hell he could grab her hips and dry hump her until he was shooting in his jeans. Because there was no way he'd make it to her pussy.

She rocked on him and his head fell forward, eyes locked with hers. She was beautiful and her body pure heaven. She moved again and his mouth went dry. He leaned forward, needing to taste her, drink from her as he worked her on his cock. When he was a hairsbreadth away from her lips, she moved back out of reach.

"You can't touch. I decide what happens."

He growled. She was his and he would have her if he wanted her. He sought her mouth out again, quicker this time, but she jerked her head away and thrust her hips forward, rubbing herself hard against his cock, moaning in apparent pleasure.

"Shit." He gritted his teeth and pushed up, forcing his dick harder against her. "Kiss me." It wasn't a request.

"No, big boy. Don't make me gag you."

He growled and thrust up so hard that he almost bucked her off him. She did not tell him what to do. She should be submitting to him. When he growled at her again, she slid off him and stood looking down at him.

"Tell me what you're feeling, Rob."

"Get back over here."

"No."

He growled again, pulling at his restraints.

"Do you want to fuck me?"

"Yes."

"How?"

"I want to mount you. Fuck you from behind. Fuck you into submission." Where the hell was his internal filter? Just because she asked didn't mean he had to confess.

"Do you want to bite me? That's how you mate."

For the love of God! "Yes."

She fell to her knees and his legs fell open on their own. "You have a beautiful cock," she murmured. Then she gently swiped her fingertip along the head, wetting her finger with his pre-come and swirling it on the slit.

"Fuck, Ariel, angel, please." He wasn't sure what he was begging for in that moment and he didn't care. The fact that he was begging in the first place didn't bother him when it should have.

She removed her finger, and his hips canted up, trying to follow the regression of her hand. When she put her finger in her mouth and sucked on it, he became mindless. Rob started pumping his hips, fucking the air. He could come just by watching her suck his essence. He didn't even have to imagine her finger was his cock and her lips were wrapped tightly around him to start shooting off. He was damn near ready just watching her.

Then she stood and quickly grasped the hem of her shirt. She pulled it off and stared at him. Jesus. She had on a lacy, see-through bra. It was so pale pink that it almost matched her supple skin. She briefly cupped her tits before pulling her pants down. Fuck! She had on matching panties. The really sexy, small, boy-short kind. He loved those.

She reached behind her back, and a second later, the flimsy material of her bra fell to the floor.

"Perfect." And she was.

"You don't think my breasts are too small?" she massaged them, pulling at her nipples, driving him fucking insane.

"Let's see if they fit in my mouth," he rasped.

She chuckled, letting her hands fall to her sides. "You're doing remarkably well."

That was totally debatable.

She straddled him again and this time, when she rocked her body against his, her arousal assaulted his senses. He could smell nothing but her. Her need was pouring into him, seeping into his very being, and his lion howled at the surface to break free and give her what she so obviously ached for.

When she started moaning, he felt the vibrations in his soul and it catapulted him to the precipice. His balls drew up.

"Shit, angel, you're gonna make me come."

Suddenly, she stopped, raising herself up enough that even when he thrust up, he got no contact in return.

"Still feel in control?"

"No. I'm about to shoot all over you."

She smirked and slid down his body, landing on her knees between his legs again. She moved, her head hovering over his dick. Then she leaned down and traced her tongue along the length of it.

"Fuck!" He gritted his teeth, locked his arms and legs, thought about baseball.

"Mmm. Guess my panties are too thin. I can taste my pussy all over your cock."

"Oh God. Get my pants off. You can leave me tied up. Just fuck me. I don't have to take you. Just fuck me. Do it hard. Do it fast."

She shook her head slowly. "What kind of test would this be if I just gave you what you wanted?"

"An easy one?"

She chuckled as she sat on the floor, scooting back a little so he could see her fully. Then she spread her legs and she slipped that delicate little hand into her panties.

She shut her eyes and bit her lip on a moan, rotating her hips as she fingered herself.

"Damn, at least take your panties off so I can see your pussy."

She shook her head, keeping her eyes shut.

Then she started moving her hand quickly, moaning, thrashing her head around, gasping as her hand went lower. She moved her other hand to her panties and moved them to the side.

"Jesus, angel. You're fucking yourself."

"So tight. Not enough." She moved her hand up and rapidly strummed her clit. "Need you."

He yanked at his binding and roared,

trying to break free, his cock leaking pro-fusely, soaking the side of his jeans.

"Oh God, Rob." She moaned, threw her head back and screamed, using both hands now, fucking herself with two fingers and assaulting her clit as she came.

He struggled at the leather holding him in place, but he couldn't take his eyes off the vision before him. He needed her. Right now!

She slumped to the floor, gasping.

"Come. Here." He was through with this little game.

She slowly looked to the side so she could see him. "You did really well. How do you feel?"

"You mean I'm *doing* well, not *did* well. We're not through. Get your sexy little ass over here."

She stood and walked toward him. She smiled and leaned down, her head going toward his cock. Not his first choice, but he was already so close to coming he'd take it. Then he'd *take* her. He was going to have to fuck her more than once tonight. Once wasn't going to be enough even after getting a blowjob. He sup-pressed a moan. The idea of her mouth encasing him sounded even better by the second.

She snagged her bra off the floor and stood up fully. "I'll have one of your brothers come in and untie you."

What that... "The hell you will," he growled. "Stop putting your clothes on."

She wasn't listening.

"You're going to seriously leave me like this? Have you ever heard of blue balls?"

"That's not the condition I'm researching." She zipped her pants and slipped into her shirt, then turned toward the door.

"Don't go!"

Ariel stopped and looked at him. "Rob, you did excellent. Don't worry. If you can keep control of yourself, we will slowly progress. Maybe next time you won't have to be tied up." She shrugged. "Well, not tied up completely. Good night."

And then she walked out the door, closing it softly behind her.

Un-fucking-believable.

———

"HOW'D IT GO LAST NIGHT?" Josh asked, chuckling as Rob dragged his ass into the dining room for breakfast. He hadn't slept a wink last night. He'd tossed and turned and jacked off so much his dick was almost raw. He was so pissed—and a little embarrassed—at how Ariel had left him that once Toby had untied him yesterday, he'd avoided his brothers the rest of the evening. Maybe he should've shifted and ran with them, burned off his aggression another way. But he didn't feel up to being razzed all night.

Jack grunted while picking up his coffee, not finding the situation amusing. He wasn't the only one. Rob grabbed a coffee cup and poured his momentary salvation before taking a seat across from Toby.

"I'm sure you all know how it fucking went." He sipped, not making eye contact with any of them.

"I'm sorry, bro. I shouldn't be teasing."

"Serves him right," Jack mumbled.

Rob looked at him, eyes narrowed, and set down his cup. "What the hell does that mean? You weren't teased to bursting, yet you still get the drugs."

"I told you she was mine. You should've stayed out of it and let me have her."

Rob was not going to go down this road.

He might be pissed with Ariel's behavior—and he knew he really had no right to be angry. She didn't do anything wrong, though his dick felt differently—but as far as he was concerned, she was still his mate. He'd just have to show her this ridiculous testing wasn't necessary. "Dude, it was her choice." He looked at Josh and picked up his cup. "Do you need me on the burnout hole?"

"Yeah. Jack is still working south side, and I have to work in the office this morning. Caldwell's daughter is trying to stir up shit again. God, that woman is maddening. At least she's willing to meet with me on Skype and has stopped demanding to come out here and meet face-to-face."

Jeffery walked in carrying two large platters filled with eggs, bacon, and biscuits. Thomas walked in as the food was placed on the table. His dad started making his plate, and then Rob and his brothers dug in.

"I heard you did well yesterday, Robert," Thomas said. "Ariel said you showed no signs of primal aggression."

"Maybe he's impudent," Jack muttered around a biscuit.

"You think you could do better in that situation, hotshot?" Toby said, coming to Rob's defense.

"I know I could." Jack squared his shoulders.

"Boys. This is unnecessary and the very reason why I had Ariel choose. Now settle down." He'd get no argument out of Rob. Jack was still being a jackass and would probably continue to be until this testing torture was finished and he was able to leave the grounds a free man.

The door opened and a very groggy-looking Mikaela walked in still in PJs. Josh dropped his fork and stood up. "What are you doing up, kitten? I thought you were going to sleep in." He started around the table toward her.

"I woke up and wanted a bite to eat." She met him halfway and gave him a peck on the lips.

Josh guided her to a chair beside him, and he fixed her plate.

"Don't let me interrupt," she mumbled into the glass of orange juice Jeffery had placed in front of her. "If I know this group, you all are giving Rob a hard time for doing what was asked of him yesterday. What he's doing is very important." Her tone held a little bit of admonishment and Rob fought a smile.

"Yeah, he's indulging a cock tease," Jack said mentally.

"I can hear you," Mikaela said, cutting her eyes in his direction. "Don't you think it's time to let go of this macho crap and be grateful there's now light at the end of your tunnel?"

Jack gritted his teeth, a small growl working up his throat as he stared at her.

Josh growled loudly and everyone looked at him. He was staring daggers at Jack. "Don't you ever growl at my wife!"

Jack cleared his throat and looked down, signaling his submission to Josh on this point. Smart man. One thing Rob understood and was just beginning to fully understand was never to jeopardize another man's mate. "I apologize, Mikaela." Jack started to rise.

"Just a minute, son," Thomas said. "Jeffery needs to administer the next round of medication before you head out." He looked at Rob. "You too."

Rob drank the last of his coffee while Jack got his shot. Then he got up from the table and walked over to Jeffery, tugging the side of his pants down for access to his hip. The chill of the alcohol swab caused goose bumps, but the sting of the needle quickly won in the discomfort category.

"Ariel will let you know when she's ready to begin your next round of tests."

"Great." Rob rolled his eyes. More tests.

"Look at it this way, son," Thomas said, lowering his voice. "You get through this, you'll be free to take excursions, visit old friends, make new friends, enjoy the world without worrying about your nature. You just have to do whatever Ariel needs to ensure the medication is virtually flawless. Your sacrifice now will pave the way for your future. And when Ariel is gone, you'll be a free man."

He'd always wanted to experience life as an adult outside this estate. To do all the things his father suggested. But now that he'd met Ariel, his goals, aspirations had shifted. He had to find a way to convince her that he was the man for her without freaking her out. No woman in her right mind would believe in love at first sight. And maybe he didn't love her as a man yet.

Maybe it was just his lion that latched onto its mate and he had to develop those feelings more naturally.

Either way, he knew if Ariel did leave once her testing was complete, he wouldn't be a free man.

Because even if she found a cure to control his animalistic urges, he would forever be a victim of his own heart.

"I need these results back as soon as possible," Ariel said, utilizing the speaker on her cell phone while she packaged the swab she'd had Josh take of Rob's saliva before she conducted her test yesterday.

And what a test that was. Knowing she had to tempt him and actually doing it proved to be two entirely different scenarios. In her mind, she'd kept complete control of the session and had not been turned on by the acts that necessitated her research findings.

In reality, she'd been so wet, so aching with need, she almost climbed onto his lap and rode him to oblivion, test be damned. She rationalized it by thinking she was a woman and he was a man. A very sexy, masculine, dreamy man, but still a man nonetheless. She hypothesized that any woman in that same situation would experience the same results. It was a chemical reaction in her body to his. It was nature. Biological and chemical.

It wasn't attraction. She would not allow herself to become attracted to Rob. She was a professional for crying out loud. And she couldn't fall in love if love didn't exist.

"DNA analysis takes a while. You know that, Ariel."

"I'm aware of it, but it's prudent to my current research, so your timeliness is greatly appreciated."

"It'd help speed things along if you tell me what you're looking for."

"It's confidential, Max." The man was a long-time colleague and sometimes friend to her. He was a bit of a hermit, but he was incredibly smart. Ariel trusted the work he did, and she needed his expertise on the Woods DNA. Since they shifted into animals, their DNA might prove some connection to why and how. It was a start.

"I'll see what I can do. I can email you a

report of my findings rather than snail mail it to you."

"That'd be great. Thanks."

After a few more niceties, she ended the call and grabbed the package. The guys were out working on the estate, so she figured Krista and Mikaela would have their noses in law books at the main house. She trekked over there, admiring the scenery on her short walk. It really was very calming out here. She wasn't much of a country girl, but she didn't fancy herself a city girl either. She was a skinny nerd. Krista was the curvy one, though she wondered if her sister had been more on the naïve side than she was. Ariel hadn't had many boyfriends before meeting Will, but that was definitely a serious relationship that led to marriage. She wondered if Krista had been in anything serious before meeting Toby. Not that it mattered now. They seemed totally smitten with each other.

Ariel smiled, thinking of her sister falling in love, and then immediately frowned. Love was a state a mind. Not a reality. It would not do for her to ever forget that.

Once she reached the main house, she

sought out the office. She heard heated voices as she neared, but couldn't quite make out the discussion. She cringed, hoping it wasn't about her and the test from yesterday.

"She cannot work here," Josh said to his wife.

Oh crap, they were talking about her. She needed to defuse the situation. No way was she going to leave before she was through with Rob. Er, before she was through with testing medication, she corrected in her thoughts.

"I think that should be my call to make," Ariel said. Josh and Mikaela turned to her and Krista looked up from reading a really thick book.

"With all due respect, Ariel, it's too soon for us to allow it. The guys are too dangerous." He turned to his wife, a pleading look in his eyes. "Besides, I don't fucking want her here."

Okay, that hurt. Ariel knew her presence here was difficult for everyone, but Josh's words were too harsh to swallow. She cleared her throat and tried squaring her shoulders, but she felt like a rabbit taking on a wolf. *A mountain lion's more like it.*

"Look, I'm sorry if I'm making things difficult being here. I promise I will try to be as expedient as logically possible—"

"Wait." Josh turned to her, shaking his head. "I wasn't talking about you. God, I wouldn't be that cruel." He sighed. "It's Caldwell's daughter, Lillian, that's demanding a job since we, and I quote, 'took her father's land out from under her.'"

Mikaela walked up to her husband and rubbed his arm affectionately. "Sweetie, let's just put her off for now. Tell her we are looking into possibly hiring new people in a few months and we'd be glad to consider her then."

"If you reject employment because she's a woman, she can sue you. It's discrimination," Krista said, not looking up from what had to be a law book in her lap.

"It's not that I think her being a woman makes her incapable of working here. It's just too dangerous with Rob and Jack."

"I know that, Josh. We all know that, but we can't tell her that. Just tell her it'll be a few months before we're ready to hire anybody."

"But I want some help now, kitten."

"If you hire someone now and she finds

out, she can make a stink," Krista said, finally looking up. "If you tell her you've already hired someone but didn't actually hire a person until later, then she can still scream foul. I think your best bet is to consider hiring her for something that wouldn't cause her to interact with the other guys and tell her that she has to earn your trust before you bring her in to the company completely."

Josh growled. "So I'll be throwing away money on her when she's not really working?"

"Maybe you can have her work her father's old land, the part that borders their property. It can be her probationary work. If she does well, then we can bring her on. By then the meds should be fully tested." Mikaela looked at Ariel. "Right?"

Crap. Ariel hated giving timelines on projects. Not that she didn't like deadlines, but because something always happened that pushed back those original dates, making her look incompetent. She took a deep breath, considering her response. "I think it's highly likely everything will be completed by then. However, this process could essentially be going on indefinitely.

We have no way of knowing at this point if the men will become tolerant of one of the chemicals in the compound. Immunity could happen quickly or over years. Or it may never be an issue. It's really too early to tell."

"Then what do you suggest?" Josh asked, arms crossed but eyes soft, genuinely seeking her opinion.

"I think it's a risk you have to assess yourself, but if Rob and Jack haven't ever worked over there and you keep them from that area of your estate, then I don't see the harm. Technically she's been over there all these years anyway, I presume. It's never been an issue before, right?"

"True," Josh muttered, nodding. Then he turned to his wife. "Okay, let me think on this. We'll try to work something out, but I want to make sure all the Is are dotted and Ts are crossed before I bring her on." He looked over at Ariel. "I'm sure I don't have to tell you the sooner you work out any bugs the better it'll be for every-one...but I'm gonna." He half-smiled at her.

"Understood." She handed a package over to him. "I actually came in to have this shipped. It's part of the research," she added quickly when he frowned at her.

"I'll make sure Jeffery takes it with him when he runs into town later."

"Thanks." She started for the door. "I need to get back to work. Um, is Rob too busy to help me?" She felt her face get hot and couldn't elaborate on just what she was expecting from Rob. Although she knew everyone in this room had to know what she was talking about.

Josh chuckled. "Rob's number one job right now is to be at your beck and call. I would say go easy on him, but you just do what you gotta do."

"Right, okay. I'll see you guys later. Maybe at dinner." She shrugged as she left. Honestly, she didn't know if they'd make it to dinner. Her next test was sure to push all Rob's buttons.

Ariel quickly walked back to her cabin, not really taking in her surroundings like she'd done before. It was hard to focus on other things when her mind was racing, preparing her for her next seduction. God, if her biochem professor could see her now.

She pushed open the rustic door to her cabin and left it ajar. She pulled out the restraints she'd used yesterday on Rob, but as she stared at them, she knew she wasn't going to use them. Josh needed her to finish her research as quickly as possible and she couldn't do that if she was too scared to move forward. Keeping Rob tied up would only serve to keep her sanity regarding her safety and not further the testing along. Tossing them aside, she quickly grabbed her cell and selected Krista's number.

"Ariel? Everything okay?"

"Yeah, yeah." Why was she whispering? She cleared her throat. "I need you to contact Rob, have Toby do it if necessary, but I need Rob to think I've suffered some kind of crisis. Minor crisis. I don't want to freak him out completely. Maybe tell him I called you because my bathroom door is stuck or something. In fact, yeah, let's go with that."

"You sound funny. Are you sure you're okay?"

"Just peachy." She was trying to tamp down her nerves. She'd never had to seduce a man before starting this with Rob. Frankly, it made her feel like a novice, and she hated feeling inferior in any regard.

"Have Toby tell him something like I'm stuck in the bathroom and need help."

"And why wouldn't Toby just come out and help you. If you call me because you're trapped, I wouldn't sit idly by. This is lame."

"Shut it, Krista. Toby can come up with something. Hell, he can tell Rob that you're freaking out and heading my way and that he needs to get to you to make sure you don't do anything stupid like wield a chainsaw and get yourself hurt. It's just a stuck door, so he can put it off on Rob."

Krista harrumphed. "I guess that'll work. Still sounds silly. You should just call him and tell him to meet you for your next booty session."

"For the love of God, Krista. I'm doing this for *you*. And I don't tell you how to do your job. Stick to the law and let me handle this the way I see fit."

Her sister sighed. "You're right. I'm sorry. I just don't like your approach to this, but I'm shutting up now. I'll call Toby. Consider it done."

"Thanks."

She tossed her cell down after ending the call and walked into the bathroom. She looked around the room, searching for something that might wedge the door shut but not having any luck. She ran to the bedroom and grabbed the small chair by the bed. It'd have to do. She just needed something to hold momentarily. She dashed back into the bathroom and propped it underneath the door handle. Then she turned on the water and shed her clothing while it heated. Once the temperature was nice and hot like she preferred, she turned on the shower and stepped in. Deciding she would actually use this time wisely, she quickly washed her body and hair.

She heard stomping feet just before a shout. "Ariel!"

She turned off the water and grabbed a towel, patting herself dry and just barely getting the towel around her body before the bathroom door shook. She heard a bang from the other side of the door just as he rattled again. This time, the hinges groaned and the door splintered.

Holy shit. Rob was sweating and panting and dirt streaked down his face, but he was a god. How could a dirty man, sweating in flannel, with wind blown hair look as hot as this? Her belly tingled and she gripped the towel tighter.

He looked at the door and frowned at the chair. Then he looked up at her, eyes narrowing. "Toby said—"

"It doesn't matter what Toby said." She leaned down and turned on the shower again. "You're filthy and I just showered. Strip."

"Excuse me? I'm working. I get dirty, angel." He crossed his arms.

"And I'm working too. You seem to be doing okay so far. We're going to take it up a notch. I need you to take off your clothes and get in the shower."

He slowly reached for the top button on his shirt. "More torture, huh?"

"If you like."

"You gonna watch?" he asked, eyebrows raised as he held open the top of his shirt.

"If I like."

He hummed in the back of his throat but continued to remove his shirt. Holy hell in a hand basket, the manual labor he must've been doing just before he ran in here caused his muscles to grow menacingly.

"You're dripping wet."

"Maybe you can do something about that later." She knew he was referring to the water still sluicing off her skin, but she couldn't pass up the innuendo.

He shut his eyes, his jaw ticking. "You're fucking teasing me again," he said through gritted teeth.

"But you're not tied up now, are you? Progress." She shrugged.

He growled, sounding a little bit pissed and a whole lot scary, but Ariel stood her ground. He unzipped his pants and pushed them down, underwear and all.

And he was hard and leaking already.

"I see my brusque tone hasn't cooled your ardor."

"You're wet and naked under that towel, angel. Your clipped tone is only making me want to subdue you even more." He stepped closer to her, invading her space and trapping her against the counter. "My nature is to make you submit to me, and you're ordering me around like a little fucking puppy. You keep this shit up and I'm going bite back."

No matter how hard she tried, Ariel couldn't contain the shiver of desire that crawled down her spine. *It's just a natural response of a woman to man.*

"Is that what you want? To bite back?" she asked breathlessly.

"Angel, you make it through this testing shit without becoming my mate and it'll be a fucking miracle. I want nothing more than to make you mine forever."

Then Rob swore under his breath, a look of pained regret in his eyes, and whirled, getting into the shower and slamming the glass door closed.

Ariel felt a pang of sadness at Rob's sudden withdrawal, but she refused to analyze why.

Some things are best left unexplained.

CHAPTER SIX

Rob scrubbed his skin like cleaning it would clean his soul. What the hell was wrong with him? He knew his animal wanted to claim her, but he had no intention of voicing that. At least not when he was considered lucid under this medication. It was almost as if in that moment, his lion had control of everything and it was only through sheer will alone he kept from crushing his mouth to hers. He guessed that was because the medication he'd been shot up with was working, but at what cost? And how well did it actually work if his lion was able to overpower him, if only for a few seconds?

The door to the shower opened and his head snapped in that direction.

Shit, shit, shit. Ariel was naked. And she was stepping into the shower with him. Fuck. He so didn't need the temptation right now, which he guessed was exactly her reasoning why now was the time to test his will. He groaned, squeezing his eyes shut and trying to force out the image of her waiflike figure out of his mind.

"Rob," she breathed, and touched his arm. His eyes opened and the compassion he saw in them almost brought him to his knees. "We'll go slow. If you want me to stop, just say the word. Okay?"

He blinked the water from his eyes and ran his hand through his wet hair, watching her, gauging her. "The problem is, angel, I don't want to stop. And you're going to."

"Yes." It wasn't a question, but she'd answered him anyway.

He shut his eyes again, trying to find the strength to resist the need, but when something hot and wet encased his dick, he gasped, eyes flying open.

"Oh fuck," he breathed, watching as Ariel took him into his mouth. She was on her knees before him and he had to grab the side of the wall with one hand to keep from digging into her scalp. With the other, he adjusted the showerhead so she wouldn't be pounded with water. It was instinctual to make sure she was protected, and he didn't fight that reaction.

Her mouth was like heaven and hell. The sweetest feeling he'd ever experienced and the most dangerous, the most tempting. He warred with himself to shove her down on the shower floor and take her verses being still and enjoying her mouth on him.

He couldn't help it. He slid his hands into her hair, knotting his fingers in her soft locks while he started to thrust into her mouth. She moaned around him, taking him deep and then swallowing. He shouted, squeezing her hair tighter. But she let his dick slip free from her welcoming heat.

"Let go."

He groaned, fingers flexing convulsively, not wanting to let her go. He slowly shook his head.

"You let go right now, or it stops."

He growled at her and her eyes got wide.

"Rob? Are you okay? What's my name?" The tremble in her voice stabbed at his heart and he unlocked his fingers from her hair without giving it another thought. He rubbed his fists in his eyes, trying to breathe through his need.

"Ariel," he rasped, answering her.

"Do you want to stop?"

Oh God, if she stopped now, he might just die right there. If she didn't think he could do this, she might think him weak and not want to do it again. Or worse. Turn to Jack. He growled. No fucking way would he let that happen. "No," he said a little too harshly, but at the moment, it couldn't be helped.

"Look at me."

Rob opened his eyes and his mouth went dry. She was sitting on the shower floor, her legs spread where he could see her beautiful pussy. She tweaked her nipples, watching him, a soft moan escaping her supple lips. He groaned, starting to move toward her. He needed to touch her, smell her, taste her.

"No, Robbie. Stay there. Just watch."

"Shit, angel." He fisted his hands but stayed put. Then the little vixen's hands slipped from her breasts to her legs, one resting on her thigh, the other diving right for her core. "Son of a bitch," he groaned as she started to masturbate. His cock was hard as steel and aching for the attention it had lost.

"You can touch yourself. Let me see you stroke that beautiful cock, Robbie."

He gritted his teeth as he complied, taking his dick in hand and roughly jacking from root to tip. She moaned, her head falling back on her shoulders as she started playing with her clit.

"Fuck, you're so hot," he growled, roughly jerking with one hand and squeezing his balls with the other. "I can come from this vision every day of my life."

She looked at him then, eyes tempting him, drawing him to her. Then she moved her hand from her pussy and sucked on her fingers, moaning.

"No fair," he panted, still working his prick.

"Tastes so good. Almost as good as you."

He groaned, shaking his head, fighting the need to...come? Take? He didn't know. He was just fighting some internal battle he didn't have time to identify.

Then she shoved her hand between her legs again and within seconds, she was screaming, writhing on the floor, thrusting her hips up in the air as she came. The sight was so erotic he stilled, mesmerized by the beauty of his mate taking her own pleasure. When she sighed and sat up, looking at him, he squeezed his dick painfully and began to fuck his fist with raging need. He was going to come and shoot all over her, her breasts, her tummy, her pussy. He was going to mark her everywhere.

"Stop."

He growled at her, shaking his head and working his fist faster. The hell he was going to stop. Fuck that.

"Rob, I said stop. You don't get to come."

He dropped his dick like it was hot coal and roared at her, crouching down and growling in her face. She squeaked. He knew he scared her, but he couldn't stop.

"Your fangs."

He licked his teeth and sure enough, his fangs had descended. Did that mean his lion was trying to take her or was it because he was too pissed to focus?

She moved slowly toward him on her knees. She softly rubbed her hands up and down his thighs like she was gentling him. Then to his surprise, she licked his cock.

"You don't...I mean...I'm sorry I..." He couldn't make out a clear thought. He didn't know what he was feeling. He didn't want her to do anything that made her uncomfortable, but he was aching for her. He needed her to make him come. He just couldn't bear the thought of making himself come again after she left like he'd had to do yesterday.

"Shh." Her lips wrapped around him and she swallowed him. He yelped at the sudden intensity of her mouth on his very sensitively aware dick, his hand clutching her shoulders in an effort to keep from holding her head like he'd done earlier.

"So good," he moaned over and over, gently thrusting his hips, trying not to overpower her. "Please don't stop, angel. Please, please don't stop." He didn't care that he was begging. He'd beg his mate every day if he had to. He never wanted the sweet heaven of her mouth to ever leave him.

She reached up and gently squeezed his balls. He spread his legs a little more to give her better access, but was constrained by the size of the shower to move too much.

It didn't matter. She fondled him one last time before moving back and massaging his perineum. He groaned, squeezing her shoulders, but trying not to hurt her, his thrusts becoming a little more demanding.

Then she pressed her finger at his pucker and instinct took over. He bore down until she breached him, shouting as she entered him and sought his prostate.

Right fucking there!

He roared, his thrusts turning frantic, and then she used her hand and mouth in tandem on his dick, moaning around him while she assaulted his sweet spot.

He couldn't hold back. God, it was too good. "You're gonna make me cooome... Oh, fuuuck!" He released her shoulders, one fist flying into the tiled wall beside him and the other reaching out to grab the bar on the shower door because instinctively, he knew if he didn't let go of her, he'd bruise her, hurt her. And that was unacceptable.

She continued to swallow him as he shot down her throat, taking his seed and his strength with him. When he had nothing left to give, he collapsed to his knees before her and took her into his arms, his lips crushing hers. He didn't care if she thought this was just a test. He had to taste her, and the temptation of his seed in her mouth was too much to resist.

She tasted of his musk and something much sweeter and he was immediately addicted. It was a taste he'd never forget and always crave. When she pulled away, he dropped his forehead to hers, breathing hard.

"Thank you, angel. I know you didn't plan for that to happen, but I, um, just thanks." He couldn't tell her what he wanted to tell her. If she truly knew he had no intentions of ever letting her go, she might bolt right now. He had to be careful if he stood a chance of winning her heart.

"The pleasure was all mine," she whispered.

He disagreed, but said nothing. It was safer that way.

———

ARIEL STARED at herself in the little blue negligee she'd brought with her, finding the strength for this next test. God, she knew this didn't conform to any professional or ethical standards, but she was having a hard time remembering that. After the shower incident yesterday, she'd stayed away at dinnertime, trying to gather her thoughts. She couldn't explain the draw she had to Rob, but she knew if she'd continued with this next step last night, she'd have thrown all ethics out the window and just fucked him. She couldn't do that. If she slept with Rob then there was no way not to become emotionally attached.

Which was *not* the same as falling in love. It couldn't be since love was just a state of mind.

But if she became attached to him, she wouldn't be able to maintain her objectivity. Therefore, she needed a little reprieve before continuing with her temptation testing.

But she was beginning to wonder who she was testing more, her or Rob. The last years of her marriage to Will had been methodical at best, so this uncharted territory with Rob sparked something deep inside her. It didn't matter. She had a job to do, and she was going to do it.

From the reports she was getting from Thomas on Jack, he was doing well with the medication. Of course, he wasn't being tested like Rob, but it relieved Ariel that Jack wasn't experiencing any adverse side effects. It gave her room to focus solely on Rob.

She'd made dinner plans with him for tonight. It'd been over twenty-four hours since she'd last laid eyes on him, and she was feeling antsy. Did that mean she missed him? She hoped not. She tried to tell herself that it was her work she missed. But she figured Rob needed this time away, too. She didn't need to push him too hard. It wasn't like every single woman he encountered would drop to her knees and suck his dick or even tempt him subtly. If he did this well with her aggressive tactics then he could survive in a world with less overbearing women.

The thought of Rob being with another woman made her heart race and a cold sweat break out. Maybe it just meant she was possessive of what this man could do for her sexually. It didn't have to mean anything more.

Surely it didn't.

The soft knock on the door brought her out of her reverie. She took a deep breath and strode over to it, channeling a self-confidence she did not feel. When she opened the door, her gaze landed on the snippet of chest peeking out from the few buttons Rob had left undone at the top of his shirt. She swallowed, trying to find the saliva that suddenly dissipated. Lord, the man was sex on a stick. Sinewy and tanned from working outside with an aura of barely contained beast radiating around him. Her eyes traveled south as she took him in. His jean-clad thighs flexed under her perusal and she had a sudden urge to rub them. She refrained. Realizing she should make eye contact, she started to look up, but the sight of his dick, hard and straining in his jeans, made her gasp and rather than look up slowly at him, her head snapped up.

Rob's eyes were narrowed, his jaw working as he seemingly ground his teeth. "You're practically naked."

Right. The little nightie. She licked her lips. "I'm covered in all the areas that matter." She turned to head toward the kitchen, and the groan she heard from Rob reminded her of what the backside of this ensemble looked like. It was lacy blue with a matching thong, but where the front hung down just past her pussy, the hem gathered up toward the back, leaving her ass completely exposed. She looked over her shoulder, but was too intimidated to look directly into his eyes. "I hope you like spaghetti."

She heard the door shut behind her, the click of the lock almost deafening. She gathered some plates and started scooping the pasta onto one when she felt his hands stroke her arms gently. She shivered at his touch and cursed herself for responding so quickly to him.

"You look beautiful," he whispered in her ear, his breath heating her skin. Then his lips found her neck and she wasn't sure how she managed to put the plate on the counter instead of letting it crash to the floor.

Ariel tilted her neck, giving him better access as she told herself it was a natural impulse because this wasn't supposed to be happening. Tonight, she'd planned on testing his will power without ever actually touching each other. Maybe she should've started with this test first. Too late to worry about that now.

"The test tonight is temptation without touching," she panted. Oh crap, he was squeezing her sides and grinding his cock against her butt cheeks as he continued to kiss and nip at her neck.

His mouth moved to her ear, and his hot breath fanned her overly sensitive skin. "Then I fail."

She only had a moment of shock at the guttural sound of his voice before he whipped her around and crushed his mouth to hers. His kiss was rough, his scruffy beard growth abrading her face while his hands fisted in the nightie that adorned her body. God, he was so raw, so animalistic that she was totally lost in him. The little noises that sounded as if they'd come from deep within him vibrated against her, making it difficult for her to continue resisting, but his humming turned into a growl when his wicked finesse wasn't pushing her into complete submission. He bit at her lips when his tongue didn't get the entry it demanded.

"Let me in." He shoved his leg between hers, rubbing his thigh at her core, and she moaned as heat flooded her. He took advantage of her weakness, sliding his tongue in as she made that needy sound. And she didn't have the desire to even try to stop him. He tasted of scotch and man and she was getting drunk off his kisses.

Her world tilted as she found herself lifted into his arms and being carried across the room.

To the bed.

And she still didn't care about right and wrong. She needed him as much as he seemed to need her. *I'm just horny.* Although that wasn't the clinical term for her current state of mind. Her body demanded, and she was powerless.

She landed softly on the bed, his mouth still on hers, insistent. His hands explored her body, but didn't touch her breasts or her pussy, driving her need higher, making her want him even more than she thought possible.

"Have to taste you," he grunted against her mouth before kissing his way south. Mercifully, one of his hands finally found her breast and she arched into his touch, moaning his name. "That's it, angel. So responsive. All mine."

Mine? Before she could contradict that statement, Ariel felt a tug against the top of her negligee, and then it disintegrated as it was torn from her body. He sucked one nipple into his greedy mouth and any protest of his claim died on her lips.

Rob ravished her breasts, pulling and tugging on one while he kissed and sucked the other, alternating between the two, making her clit want the same attention. She lifted her hips, trying to make contact, needing to ease the ache that was growing in her.

He tore his mouth away and stared down at her. Gazing into her eyes, he slowly thrust himself against her, grinding his cock into her core as he watched her closely. His intent stare was tender in a way, yet seemed to see right into her very soul, pulling at her defenses and controlling her need with his masterful body.

And he still was completely dressed. The fact that this man could make her want, make her crave, make her *need* beyond all rational thought with only his mouth and hands on her was shocking. Maybe if she got him to remove his clothing, it'd level the playing field somewhat. As long as he stayed dressed, he would keep the upper hand.

She needed that rectified right now.

"Your clothes need to come off," she

whispered, trying to emulate the stare he was giving her but feeling as though she sorely lacked the same ability.

"Yes," he breathed.

He pushed himself against her one last time before sitting on his knees and unbuttoning his shirt, and Ariel wondered how it was scientifically possible for a man to have this perfect of a body. When he sat up and unbuttoned his pants, she could do nothing but lay there and watch, paralyzed by this powerful presence. He managed to get his pants and underwear down with little maneuvering, so when his cock sprang free, her mouth watered as she remembered the taste of him.

"Not now, angel. It's my turn." Her panties received the same fate as her nightie, and the scraps of material were tossed to the floor as he descended. He inhaled, groaning against her pussy, and she couldn't help but wiggle, her body making the plea for her. He grasped her thighs, shoving them wider apart, and then licked her from ass to clit.

"Oh God, Robbie. That feels, ahh..." He stabbed his tongue into her, fucking her with his mouth as he groaned, the vibrations better than any vibrator she'd ever used before. She gasped, and he shoved his tongue into her faster and brought his thumb down to torment her clit, rubbing circles around it, but not touching it directly. She was so close to coming already that she didn't know if she wanted him to rub her sweet spot yet, or if she should try to hold out. If she could wait, then maybe she wouldn't seem like a whimpering, aching mess of a neglected woman. She clamped her lips shut when she felt like she couldn't control the begging from coming out. She fisted the sheets and stiffened her legs, trying to hold off the inevitable.

Rob growled, squeezing her thighs with bruising strength, then suddenly wrapped his lips around her clit and sucked, batting it with his tongue while he knifed two fingers inside her. She screamed as stars exploded behind her eyelids, her body quaking with the force of her orgasm. He continued his ministrations while she flew and eased back on the intensity as she came off that magical high. When he stopped, she couldn't find the strength to open her eyes, even when she heard him rummaging around in the nightstand beside her or when she felt him come over her.

"Open your eyes. Look at me, angel." The soft command brooked no argument. When she obeyed, she had to stifle a gasp. Rob looked at her as if she were his whole world and what they were about to do would be the start of something great. She shivered, not understanding if it was fear of that possibility or excitement.

He clutched her knee, moving her leg in the process, and hooked it around his hip. When she looked down at his cock in his hand, poised at her entranced, she noticed he'd put on a condom, realizing that was what he'd probably been searching for in the nightstand.

He pushed into her slowly, letting go of her knee and his cock at the same time and propping himself up above her. He panted, and she gyrated beneath him, trying to entice him to push into her fully. He felt hard and thick, but she was too wanton to care if it'd hurt.

His head fell to her neck on a groan. "Stop, angel. Lemme work it in." He started rocking against her, pushing into her in increments that only drove her crazy. She reached up and grabbed his ass while wrapping both legs around his hips, pulling him toward her. "Fuck, fuck!"

"Yes!" She thrust against him and rotated her hips, inviting the sting of being fully penetrated.

It was enough to unleash his beast. Well, not technically—he was still fully human, but he sank down on top of Ariel, slid his hands underneath her shoulders to hold her in place, and then he started pounding into her. She clawed at his back, seeking purchase, and anchored her knees against his waist. And just felt. Felt Rob fuck her, possess her, own her.

Take her.

With that thought, heat flooded her core and her vagina convulsed around his cock as she flew into her second orgasm.

"Fuck me, you feel like heaven." He licked a line from her neck to her ear and sucked on her lobe. "Again," he demanded. Rob shifted his angle and thrust into her harder, faster, and she was powerless to deny him. Her body was his to command, and she gave him what he ordered, this time screaming as she came.

He shouted, riding through her peak,

and still he was relentless. He pulled out and dove, his mouth latching onto her pussy, and he mauled her as he ate at her again. She didn't think it was possible, but he was determined to wring every climax her body had to give. It took longer this time, her body shaking with indecision, not knowing if she could do it again but aching for it. When she finally came, she felt as if her body reached a state of euphoria unlike any other, the high the sweetest experience of her life. Barely aware, she felt her body turning as Rob placed her on her hands and knees, and when he entered her again, she was still coming from before. He pounded into her with near brutal force, and all she could do was ride the high. She heard a hoarse-sounding cry and realized it was her. She'd screamed so much that her throat was hurting.

Then with a roar that shook her, she felt Rob stiffen behind her and shove impossibly deep. He lifted her up so that she was sitting on his lap and held her down onto his cock as he came, his hips jerking with the force of his climax.

When the both collapsed onto the bed, Ariel was so physically and mentally exhausted that she couldn't fight the sleepiness that was coming over her.

The last thing she heard was Rob whispering to her as he stroked her arm.

"You are so amazing. Rest, my beautiful ma..."

The rest was lost in the darkness.

CHAPTER SEVEN

WAKING up with Rob's body cocooning hers made Ariel feel like melting into him a little more. Which was exactly why she'd slithered out from the bed, threw on some clothes, and decided to work in the main house.

She wasn't an idiot.

If she'd stayed, she would've been at his mercy. Probably having more sexual relations. Granted, her body would've enjoyed it—she *was* deliciously sore this morning—but her heart, er, her head would've been fighting the attraction. And she needed her head focused on her task. A task that was not exactly why she was here, but more peripheral. She argued with herself that gaining this knowledge would help with her primary objective—stabilizing the Woods' aggressive mating needs—because it'd help her grasp everything as a whole. And it was a question that niggled at her from day one.

Where did these cat shifters come from? That was what she needed to learn. And why hadn't anyone asked this question before? As far as she thought, everyone in the know just accepted them at face value since the history of their kind died with Thomas' parents. But her scientific mind just wouldn't concede to that. She needed concrete evidence that supported one of her theories. And said theories ran the gamut of far out possibilities, which were borrowed from comic strips, Area 51, and government lab experiments gone awry. She had other less dramatic theories, like gene mutation, or infection, or a combination of both of those things, or many other theories. She knew she was grasping at straws, but she had to start somewhere.

She'd been at it for hours, locked in the office, skipping breakfast, and hadn't discovered anything to suggest any theory was superior to the others. It was frustrating because she was searching blindly, but she had no other choice. She was in the middle of reading werewolf legends when she heard the handle jiggle on the small office door.

"Brought you some food," Krista said. Mikaela followed behind her.

"I'm not hungry." Ariel turned back to the computer.

"How'd it go last night?" Krista asked as she set a plate of fruit and croissants next to her.

Mikaela snatched up a few strawberries before leaning against the desk, facing Ariel.

She sighed, turning to face her intruders. "It went fine."

"Funny," Mikaela said, lifting a piece of the fruit to her mouth. "That's exactly the same thing Rob said at breakfast."

Ariel felt her cheeks get hot and she quickly tucked her hair behind her ear, trying to hide her embarrassment. She could talk about pretty much anything in a clinical setting, but when the attention was focused on her, she felt totally inept. Just remembering how Rob had mastered her body sent a shiver of remembered need coursing through her.

"Oh my God, you slept with him!" Krista screeched.

At the scornful look in her sister's eyes, Ariel said, "Seduction is a necessary part of testing the compound." She quickly grabbed a croissant to help shove any more lame excuses from spilling out. She could lie all she wanted to herself, but vocalizing that threadbare excuse made her feel even more ridiculous.

"So you feel nothing for Rob? He's just a lab rat to you?" This was from Mikaela. Great. So now they were both ganging up on her. She needed to divert their attention and fast.

"Look, I can't explain what's happening with him, but maybe you can help me find some answers. I'm actually here trying to research their family history. If we know more about why they have the ability to shift in the first place, then treating them long term will be so much easier."

"You think we're stupid enough to fall for that evasive tactic? We're both lawyers, for crying out loud. We've seen defendants do a better job when being questioned by the prosecution." Krista crossed her arms and glared at her.

Mikaela sighed and looked at Krista. "Let's give her a break. Rob is a big boy, and he's not talking either." She glanced at Ariel. "Yes, he's not been playing *Twenty Questions* and it's pissing my husband off." Then she chucked and ate another strawberry.

Ariel took a deep breath and focused on Mikaela. It was easier than trying not to squirm under her sister's stare. "What can you tell me about their family history?"

"Well, let's see. Thomas' parents died when he was very young. He doesn't remember them. He also doesn't talk about how he was able to mate with his wife. He's very secretive about all that."

"Do you think he really knows something and is hiding it from his sons?"

Krista frowned, looking over at Mikaela. "You don't think that, do you? I couldn't imagine Thomas being that careless where his boys are concerned."

"No, I don't think it's anything like

that. If I had to guess, I think he really doesn't know anything about where he comes from. He probably stumbled into his —for lack of a better work—*heritage* and might've taken his mate in a manner he wasn't proud of, so he doesn't talk about it."

"As in...you think he might've raped their mother?" Krista paled.

"Oh, no, no, no. If he took her against her will, then they both would be dead. Remember what happened to Eric?" Ariel frowned, trying to remember the name, and Mikaela paused. "Eric was the youngest of the brothers. He mated with a woman against her will. She attacked him after she shifted and they fought to the death."

"So what keeps them from attacking any woman they mate?"

"Love. If a woman is willing to spend the rest of her life with one of them, then she wouldn't attack after being mated. The men are very primal in that state, so it's hard for them to grasp their humanity. If a woman he doesn't love is attacking him, his natural instinct is to protect himself."

Love. Ariel didn't believe in love, so how could an imaginary state of mind stop two people from killing each other? She needed something more convincing than a fanciful illusion.

"Anyway, I think Josh's parents knew each other, maybe were already sweet on each other, and Thomas mated her. You know how they get when the need to mate overtakes them. It's not all sweet kisses and flowery words." Mikaela giggled.

"And he's from a different era. Where women today might get off on being dominated, thirty years ago it probably wasn't as socially acceptable," Ariel guessed.

"Exactly. If he's ashamed of his mating, he wouldn't want to talk about it. Besides, talking about how he mated with their mother has nothing to do with how he came to be the way he and his sons are."

"True," Ariel murmured. "I need to find the missing link that connects Thomas' family to the shifters within it."

"Maybe if we sneak—"

Mikaela's sentence was cut short when the door to the office opened so hard that it hit the wall and shook the plaques hanging on it.

Ariel's mouth fell open at the sight of Rob, panting, his work clothes disheveled, his hair mussed as if he'd been tunneling his fingers through it repeatedly.

"Out," he snapped.

Ariel stood as if she were going to flee. No need to ask her twice. If her body hummed at the sight of him, she ignored it.

"Not you."

"Rob, are you okay? Do you want me to get Josh?" Mikaela asked.

Rob glanced at her. "I'm fine. I need to have a word with Ariel." He looked dead at his person of interest. "Alone."

"I'm not leaving my sister alone with you," Krista said, and Ariel envisioned her stomping her foot, but she couldn't look away from Rob's gaze to see if that theory were true.

"Toby knows I'm here too."

As if on cue, Krista's cell phone buzzed, and she pulled it out of her pocket and read the screen. "Let's go," she sighed, looking at Mikaela. Then she looked at Ariel. "We're not going far."

Ariel watched, stunned, as her only source of protection left her in the lion's den with one seemingly pissed off kitty cat.

"Care to explain yourself, little one?"

———

ROB WAS SHAKING he was so angry. They'd had a night filled with passion. His need had exploded around them, and Ariel had been right there with him every step of the way, begging, responding, coming apart in his arms over and over again.

Until he'd woken up alone in her bed with an erection that was so hard he could pound nails with it. Where his little waif had run off to, he didn't know, but before he could storm out in search of her, Josh had cock blocked him. His older brother had stopped him from hunting his mate down and sternly suggested Rob give her some time to adjust. His brother had smelled her all over him, so there was no pretending nothing had happened, but that didn't mean Rob had to provide any details —no matter how hard Josh had tried to get some answers.

So Rob had done what was expected of him. He went to breakfast. Alone. And began his workday. Irritated. He'd had every intention of leaving Ariel to her research or whatever she needed to do while she was away from him, but as the seconds ticked by and the minutes dragged on, he found himself more worked up. It was only midmorning, and he couldn't fight the need to seek her out. He had to find out why she'd snuck out on him. Yes, he was agitated because of her, but he was furious with himself for not being able to go a few hours without going to her.

"W-what do you mean?" She backed away a few steps and his lion wanted to pounce.

"Stop moving back! I'm so on edge that I won't be able to resist the chase," he gritted out, fisting his hands in an effort to stay immobile.

"Sorry," she gasped, and took a tentative step toward him. He breathed a little easier. She wasn't near close enough, but at least she'd stopped her retreat.

"Why did you leave me?"

Ariel took another hesitant step closer, and Rob released his fists, stretching out his fingers. "I have work to do, Rob. I can't stay in bed all day."

"I woke up at five a.m. and you were already gone. That's hardly sleeping in, Ariel."

"Um, I know that I—"

"Were you afraid of getting fucked again this morning? Because, angel, you would have been." He had to touch her. He moved slowly toward her. "I would have rolled you on your back and slid deep inside you. Kissed you lazily while I took my time building your pleasure up." He reached for her, pulling her into his arms, his mouth finding her ear. "But now, I just want to bend you over that desk and fuck you like a rutting animal. Show you who you belong to."

She squeaked when he crushed his mouth to hers, but the sound morphed into a moan as she wrapped her arms around his back. Rob's internal voice screamed in victory. She wanted him and he needed her. Right fucking now.

He broke the kiss and turned her so that she was facing the desk. "Keep your hands flat against the desktop." He yanked her pants and panties down with one hand while he unbuckled his pants with his other. He shoved a finger inside her and found her ready. "God, you're so fucking wet."

He pulled out his finger and pushed his cock into her.

"Rob!" Her pussy clamped down on him and he stilled.

"Shit, are you too sore, angel?" No matter how much he needed to own her in this moment, he could never hurt her. He'd rather cut his own heart out.

"It's okay," she breathed, and pushed back against him.

He groaned, conflicted with wanting to do the right thing and needing to take her...as much as he could take her right now.

"Please," she whispered, and the internal battle was decided. Rob slowly pushed the rest of the way into her moist heaven. "Yes."

Her barely vocalized acceptance was like fire licking at his balls. He came over her and thrust into her repeatedly. He wouldn't be able to hold out like he had last night. His emotions were too raw, his need too overpowering, but his lion wouldn't allow him to come before its mate. He snaked his hand around her hip and down between her legs. She yelped when he made contact with her clit and flinched away. Rob bit her shoulder to hold her in place and growled low, warning her not to resist as he strummed her clit and fucked her hard.

"You're gonna make me come," she panted.

He released her shoulder. "Do it, angel. I'm dying here." When her pussy began to flutter, he knew she was done for. "That's it. Shit!"

She screamed, and he came inside her as he flattened her to the desk and rocked against her with his own orgasm. He bracketed her and panted, breathing in her angelic scent, a smell that would forever be burned into his very soul. He was falling in love with her. He always knew that he would. She was his mate, so love would naturally come, but to actually feel it and know it was happening, well, that was one of the greatest feelings he'd ever experienced.

When he gently released her and pulled out, he winced. "Um, angel, I'm sorry. I didn't use a condom." He knew better than this shit. He and his brothers were always to protect themselves, and Rob definitely wanted to protect his mate. But his lion didn't care. Taking her without a condom meant marking her in the most intimate way possible. Yeah, he should've known better, but it was hard to fully feel remorse.

She gasped and turned around to face him. "What?" The color fled from her face, and Rob reached for her. She jerked away from him.

"I said I was sorry and I meant it. Why are you backing away from me again?" He frowned as she kept moving back.

"Does this mean I could get pregnant now?"

Why in the hell did she look disgusted? He growled. "No."

"Are you sure? I mean, you can get women pregnant, right? Or is that not physically possible?"

"Are you fucking kidding me, Ariel? I'm a man, not a fucking creature. Just because I shift into an animal doesn't mean I'm not one hundred percent man." When she didn't say anything else right away, Rob was felt his heart dropping. *She thinks I am a creature. Not capable of being a man she needs.* His lion demanded he prove her wrong, make her see him for the person he was and not the science experiment she thought of him. But all he really wanted to do was flee. Maybe it was because of the medication that he didn't want to stay and fight. "You know what? Just forget it. I'm through with your fucking tests."

And he ran. He barely cleared the door before he shifted into the animal she would always think him.

CHAPTER EIGHT

ARIEL HAD SPENT the last week with her nose buried in one book or another, reading about the history of civilization and chemical compounds. Rob was avoiding her, and she couldn't say that she completely blamed him. After the last time they were together, she'd freaked out when he hadn't used a condom, but he'd taken it all wrong. Since her marriage to Will soured, she hadn't been using birth control. The medication had always made her sick, so she only took it if she absolutely had to. The bottom line was she wasn't protected against pregnancy and she wasn't ready to be a mom. That was all.

And the fact that she hadn't originally questioned Rob's humanity and ability to conceive like he'd assumed she was worried about made her realize he'd somehow knocked her off her game. She was a scientist, biochemist here to do a job, and the first thing that should have popped into her mind was the scientific probability of the Woods men being able to conceive. If it wasn't possible, then Rob and his brothers wouldn't be here.

But that wasn't Ariel's first concern. Over the last week, she'd tried telling herself that her reaction was a typical woman's reaction...and she was a woman. But she couldn't help but acknowledge that in such a short amount of time Rob had become more to her than a test subject. She didn't want to analyze what he was to her because she was analytical by nature and would pick it apart until she discovered the answer.

She didn't want to know the answer to that. In this case, ignorance was truly bliss, but as her days went on, she found herself not concentrating on her work, her thoughts drifting to one tall, dark, and sexy as hell man who lived in the cabin next to her. No matter how hard she tried to push him out of her mind, he'd find his way back with a vengeance.

Rob had been true to his word and not allowed any more testing, so regardless of her wishes to fully test his will, she knew that opportunity had sailed. She couldn't even bring herself to approach Jack about participating in some tests. Ariel's stomach turned with just the fleeting thought. So instead, she just formulated the drugs and gave them to Thomas to administer, and after Thomas watched them give themselves their own shots, he started leaving the syringes with them at night for them to medicate themselves in the morning, and then he'd collected the empty syringes at breakfast to return to her. It was a system that ensured the men learned how to medicate themselves without assistance and pushed her out of the equation completely. At this point, she could concoct the compound at her lab on campus and ship it to them.

She really had no reason to see Rob anymore. And that thought made it difficult for her to breathe because she knew the longer she stayed, the more difficult it'd be to walk away. This past week had been difficult enough and she knew he was close by. Her sister did her damnedest to keep her away, too, telling her how great of a cook Toby was and inviting her to dinner at their cabin every night. Krista had told her that she just wanted some quality time with her, but Ariel was smarter than that. She did appreciate the excuse to avoid dinner with everyone though. She wanted to see Rob. She just couldn't bring herself to face his wrath with an audience.

There was no denying she cared for Rob. How it happened, she had no idea, but she knew she was too gun shy to go down that road again. She didn't believe in love, and she had no intention of changing her beliefs. But that didn't negate the fact that she felt *something* for him.

It was because of those feelings that she had to make things right with Rob. She'd tried calling him, but he hadn't answered. She'd considered telling Krista what was wrong and have Toby explain it to Rob, but that had felt like a copout. She'd made this mess with him, so she needed to be the one to fix it. She needed to go to him, tell him in person. She could've done it days ago, but she was a chicken. She knew that. She fully realized once she was within his grasp again that she'd bend to his will. It wasn't love, though. It was sex. With a man she cared about. That was all.

Yes, a total chicken.

But it was time to make amends and move forward. She hadn't gotten anywhere with herself imposed semi-isolation, her researching into the Woods family connections turning up big goose eggs and the medication working with only minor tweaks.

Ariel closed the book she was reading. It was mid-afternoon, so she assumed Rob would still be out on the land, harvesting or planting trees. With no plan other than to talk to him, she left her cabin and started walking into the woods.

———

"ROB?" Josh sounded on Rob's radio.

He unclipped it from his belt and brought it to his mouth. "Yeah?"

"I have a bead on our guest. She's walking on the north end quadrant, heading to the burnout. Thought you'd like to know."

What the hell was Ariel doing walking around out here like she was on some fucking field trip? Didn't she realize there was heavy machinery and trees being extracted, and his brothers out on wheelers creating a very dangerous situation for someone unfamiliar with their work tactics? She could get hurt or worse.

"I'm on it."

Damn that little waif of his. He'd been hurt and pissed, so he'd avoided her like the plague, which proved a monumental feat. Just because he was mad didn't mean he didn't want her with aching force. He'd stayed away from his cabin during the day so he wouldn't accidentally run into her... or pretend to run into her because lord knew that ridiculously embarrassing thought had crossed his mind. God, he'd run at night with his brothers just to sleep in his feline form outside her door. He knew it was pathetic. His brothers and his father were all worried about him. In the waning hours of his medication, he couldn't resist his lion's need to be near its mate. He knew his family talked about him and about how Ariel's tests had been too much for him. Hell, they talked about that in front of him. He knew they'd witnessed him staying in his shifted form and sleeping outside, and he didn't give a shit. He was not ashamed of how she made him feel.

He just wished she thought of him as a man and not a beast.

He put down the chainsaw he'd been using to clear debris for a new trail and hopped on his wheeler. He had to go much slower than he wanted because he didn't want to startle her when he neared or actually hit her when he was upon her. When he rounded the last bend en route to the burnout hole, he slowed even more when he spotted her. She was such a sight for sore eyes. He knew he missed her, could still smell her when he was by her cabin, and got whiffs of her in the main house, but just seeing her again would've brought him to his knees if he were standing. She turned and watched him approach and it was all he could do to calmly pull up beside her and kill the engine.

"You shouldn't be out here, angel." His voiced sounded raw even to him.

She stepped closer and damn if he couldn't move away. He was trapped on the all-terrain vehicle. She put her hand on the bar beside his, not touching.

"Hi to you, too." She was smiling at him and his giddy heart started pounding. *Too fucking bad.*

"You need to head back inside or at least away from the wooded areas of the property. You know we do work out here. It's not safe for you to be lurking around."

"I'm not lurking. I'm looking."

"What are you looking for?"

Her pinky moved next to his hand and gently grazed his skin. Just that simple touch made him want her even more if that were even possible. He already ached for her night and day.

"You."

"Shit, Ariel. Why?" Oh God, please say it's because you want me.

"I owe you an apology, I think. You jumped to the wrong conclusion when we were together last, and you left before I could explain. Come to think of it, I think that means you owe *me* an apology." She chuckled.

"You're speaking in circles, angel."

"I asked about the pregnancy possibility after the no-condom scare because

I'm not ready to be a parent. It had nothing to do with you and your ability to shift. Any young woman in my situation would feel the same way."

"Your situation being that you're fucking a man who turns into an animal?" Was she just here to pour salt into his wounded heart? If so, he'd stand here and take it, but God, he'd be crushed all over again.

She moved up to him quickly and rested her hands on his chest, the heat of them scorching through his shirt. "No, Robbie," she whispered. "My situation being that I'm not on birth control. The medicine makes me ill, so I stopped taking it after Will and I stopped having sex. There wasn't a point in suffering, and I haven't given it any thought because I had no intention of engaging in sexual intercourse with you. I *did* plan on testing your sexual limits, but I did have limits of my own that you barreled over. I just didn't plan on it being an issue until we were faced with what we'd done."

"So you don't think I'm some kind of monster?" Why the hell did his voice crack? And why was he watching her as if her answer held the key to his very existence? Yet, he knew the answers to those questions. He now had a sliver of hope. Hope that maybe she did accept him for who and what he was, and he was terrified that the hope he felt would be crushed.

"No, I don't."

He moved then, clutching her hands at his chest. "I'm sorry I didn't give you a chance to explain yourself. I thought—"

"I know what you thought, and I'm sorry I wasn't strong enough to confront you before now. I did try to call—"

"I'm sorry. I know. I just couldn't answer. I was worried I'd start yelling at you and I didn't want to hurt you, no matter how much pain I was in."

She leaned into him and he wrapped his arms around her, holding her. He felt a rumble in his chest and he didn't worry that his purring would freak her out. She just held him back and stroked his arm.

"There's something else I think you should know," she mumbled against his chest.

"What's that, angel?"

"My relationship with Will left me scorned. I haven't believed in love in a long time. I'm still not convinced it exists, and I need you to know that." She moved out of his embrace and wrapped her arms around herself for protection. "I'm not saying whatever is happening between us is like that, or...or even more than some casual fun... mixed with work. I just need you to know so you won't expect something from me that I cannot give."

Rob slung his leg over the wheeler, stood up, and walked toward her before he'd even registered fully what she'd said. She felt she wasn't capable of love? Bullshit. There was no doubt in his mind she had a kind, loving soul. But she also looked timid and ready to run. He needed to handle her like he would a scared kitten.

"I'll never, ever expect more from you than what you're capable of giving me, angel." He reached up and tucked her windblown hair behind her ear. "I just want the chance to prove to you that I can be good for you. Please don't let the actions of another man ruin what we could have."

"This is just moving too fast for me." She stumbled back and Rob had to control the urge to reach out for her. She was struggling with her beliefs, and he could wait for her to be ready. She made the step to come find him. He had to believe she would come back for him again. He would wait until he took his dying breath. So he'd do the hardest thing he'd had to do since meeting the woman who would own his heart fully.

He'd let her go.

"I won't pursue you if you don't want me to." God, saying those words was like ripping his heart out while it was still beating. He went from despair to hope and then back to crushing misery. There would be no drug strong enough to dull the excruciating pain that radiated through him in this moment.

She stopped and turned. "I can't, Robbie. This is too much."

He nodded, too choked up to speak. Too weak to resist begging if he did open his mouth.

"Please," she breathed, and he was shocked to realize he wasn't the one uttering the word.

She stepped closer to him, and he didn't know what she was begging for. Did she want him to run from her? Did she want him to stay and fight? God, he didn't know what to do.

"We can go slow. Take all the time in the world to just see what happens."

"I'm scared." She swayed toward him, and he grabbed her, his greedy mouth finding hers with a desperation he knew all too well since meeting his little waif. He told himself, ordered his body to go slow like he'd just promised they could do. No way was he going to frighten her away with the forceful need coursing through him right now. He eased his kisses, turning them light and teasing while he ran his hands through her hair, just holding her to him, tasting her, drinking from her like a man enjoying the finest whiskey and not a starved man experiencing food for the first time. Easy, sipping kissing that had her clutching at his arms and moaning into his mouth.

Rob eased her to the ground, kissing her mouth and traveling down her neck, licking and lightly nipping her skin. He was hard and wanted her right now, but he had to take his time. Show her that he could be a gentle lover too.

He slid his hand up her shirt and

squeezed her breast and his mouth moved to her ear. "I love your body. So beautiful. Perfect."

Her hand slithered under his belt and into his jeans. Her soft little hand wrapped around his cock and he couldn't keep the groan from escaping his lips. He rested on his elbow and kissed her again, sliding his hand from her breast to inside her pants like she'd just done for him. He found her wet and ready and gently rubbed her clit in time with her shallow pulls of his cock.

He took his time, learning her body like he should've done before. Each time they'd been together it was fierce, all consuming, and now he'd control the burn at a heated simmer.

Ariel pulled her hand out from his jeans and started unbuttoning his shirt, kissing the exposed skin she found. He'd been working all day, so he knew he was dirty, but if she noticed, she didn't care. They slowly divested each other of the rest of their clothing and within minutes, he was easing into her welcoming body. They fit perfectly together, as if Rob had any doubt.

He made love to her on the ground in

the middle of the woods, surrounded by temptation of love, of future, of hope.

When she came, he pulled out and finished right after her, holding her, loving her. There was no doubt in his mind that he was in love with her. Maybe it'd happened the moment his lion acknowledged her as his mate. It didn't matter. But as she wrung the last of his seed from his body, his fangs descended, a new demand to take. And he was going to.

Just not today.

CHAPTER NINE

Ariel awoke to soft kisses at the nape of her neck, and she realized she was falling fast and hard for Rob. In the weeks since their misunderstanding and subsequent make up, they'd been practically inseparable. Rob slept in her cabin with her. They'd have breakfast in bed, meet for lunch together in the cabin—followed by some hot and fast sex—and then they'd eat in, begging off offers to join the others at the main house. It was as if they were living in their own little world. It was perfect.

And it scared her. The last time she had something perfect, it had been an illusion. Love was just an illusion. She'd learned that lesson the hard way. But when she was with Rob, he made her forget how reality could be and she was able to live that fantasy with him. And since they'd spent every moment possible together, she never really had time to acclimate herself with the vestiges of reality.

"Good morning, my beautiful angel," Rob mumbled against her hair as he nuzzled it. And his face wasn't the only part of him rubbing against her.

"How good is it gonna be, Robbie?" she teased.

"Oh, baby, I'm so good, I can make you beg for it." He chuckled as he continued to kiss her neck and then ground his cock against her ass. When she arched her back, moving her hips to give him greater contact, he growled playfully and rolled her over. "You're a little vixen this morning, angel." He reached into the nightstand for a condom and quickly donned it.

"How can a vixen be an angel?" she asked, giggling. Her laughter died on a moan as his lips found hers. He licked her lips, nudging them apart and then slowly slid his tongue into her mouth, lightly massaging its counterpart.

Her legs wrapped around his waist of their own volition, and since they'd been sleeping together in the nude, he had clear access to her pussy. She lifted her hips and he slid in. They both groaned at the delicious friction.

"Robbie," she moaned. "Like that. Take me, baby." His thrusting went from easy and languid to rough and fast. He started fucking her with renewed determination at her command. Rob was a vocal person, but whenever she voiced her sexual need, it never failed to get his engine running.

He growled and her eyes snapped up to his. Oh shit. His fangs were out. It wasn't the first time they'd descended during sex, or even foreplay, but that virile look in his eyes caused her to pause.

"Robbie? You okay?" She panted because he was still fucking her relentlessly.

He groaned and dug his head into the area where her shoulder met her neck. "Yeah, angel. Just. Want. You."

"You have me," she breathed, and she didn't know where that had come from.

He growled loudly, rose above her, and thrust so hard that the headboard banged against the wall with every forward progression. "Mine," he rasped. "Say it!"

She squeezed her lips shut and shook

her head, pushing at his shoulders in defiance but churning her hips to bring her closer to orgasm.

"Now, angel. Say it, damn it!" He grabbed her hair and yanked her head to the side. He lowered his head and licked the veins throbbing in her neck, but then suddenly pulled back and stared down at her. "Mine. Mine!"

She shook her head again and he hissed at her. His fangs were menacingly long.

"No, Robert," she ordered in her most authoritative voice.

He growled again and stabbed into her so perfectly that she finally flew off the precipice. When she screamed his name, he roared, but he was cut shot as he turned his head quickly away from her. She heard him whimpering as the cloud of her climax lifted.

And then she saw blood.

"Oh my God, Rob, are you okay?" She grabbed his head and made him look at her. Blood trickled down his chin and dripped onto her chest. Her eyes darted all over him, landing on his wounded arm. He'd bitten himself. Before she could ask him why, he leaped from the bed, dragging a startled cry from her when his penis left her vagina so abruptly.

He ran to the fridge, and she watched him as he pulled the capped syringe out, shaking as he fumbled with it. She rose and headed toward him to help.

"No. Stay there. I don't want to hurt you."

That made her freeze.

"Robbie, you're not going to hurt me. You just got really turned on and your fangs came out. It's happened before."

He panted as he stabbed the needle into his bare hip, and then he backed away from her as he rubbed the injection site and then ripped off the condom. "I have to go. I need to get to work."

"It's before breakfast. Your family won't be out there yet."

But her response wasn't acknowledged as he grabbed the door and ran from her cabin bare-ass naked.

———

ROB HAD SKIPPED BREAKFAST, choosing to shower first and then shift and run instead. Being with Ariel was amazing.

He was in love with her and he wanted to spend the rest of his life with her. But each time they made love, it got harder and harder for him to resist the temptation of his lion claiming her. The command she'd uttered had been the breaking point for him. He'd been loving her with care and then the moment she demanded that he take her, he wanted nothing more. To his lion, it was an offering. But he knew it was just sexual and he couldn't give in to that desire to possess her fully. So he fled at the first opportunity—after making sure he got his daily dose of docile juice. He was so revved up, he knew he'd needed all the help he could get.

After he ran for hours, he went back home to shower and get ready for work. Thankfully, he hadn't smelled Ariel in her cabin when he'd passed. Otherwise, he wasn't sure he would've been able to stop himself from going over there.

He was just arriving at his post when his radio sounded. "You there yet, Rob?"

He unclipped it from his belt and put it to his face. "Yeah, Josh. What's up?"

"You okay, man? Toby said Ariel called Krista early this morning and neither of them showed up for breakfast. Jack called and said he had to get ready for an early Skype call with Caldwell's daughter, so he bailed too. It was just me, Dad, and Mikaela."

Which meant Josh was itching to find out what had happened and hadn't gotten any answers from anyone else.

"I'm fine."

"So what happened? Why did Ariel call Krista away first thing this morning?"

"It's nothing. I need to get to work. I got a late start."

"You can tell me, you know. I've been there before." Josh sounded sincere enough that Rob sighed.

"It's hard. That's all."

"Because you want to claim her and can't?"

"How'd you..." He paused, taking a deep breath. "Yes. I want to claim her. She's my mate and it's natural for us to want that." He couldn't help the defensive edge that crept into his voice.

"Hey, you don't owe me an explanation, Rob. I know the need to take one's mate is damn near impossible to resist. Just because you're on meds to keep from tipping over the edge doesn't mean you're not faced with that edge every moment you're near her."

That was exactly it, and Rob felt like less of a failure getting this little pep talk from his older brother. "Thanks, man. I needed to hear that."

"Anytime."

"If you two lovebirds are through being all sappy on this channel," Toby cut in on the radio, "then I'd like some help."

Rob heard Josh chuckle over the airwaves. "Whatcha need, Toby?"

"Jack is M.I.A."

"What do you mean?" Josh was all serious now, no teasing tone left.

"His tractor is parked, and I'm looking down at a pile of clothes beside it. Looks like he shifted and ran."

"So?" Rob asked. He'd just shifted this morning and run. Sometimes they needed to let go of some steam and being one with nature was the best way to do that.

"So, I went to the office to meet up with Jack before coming out here to see if he wanted me somewhere specific. He wasn't there, so I checked the log on his computer to see what time his meeting ended. He never logged into Skype this morning, which means he missed his appointment with the Caldwell chick."

Rob's insides turned to ice. His fingers felt numb as he slowly brought the radio up to his mouth. "Or he lied about ever having an appointment in the first place?"

"Now why the fuck would he do that?" Josh barked.

"Because he needs an alibi," Rob mumbled, foreboding prickling his skin.

"Son of a bitch! Josh, this isn't good. There are fucking needles here. I kicked his clothes around and they fell out. Looks like the shit that fucker is supposed to be taking for his aggression. And they're still full."

"Ariel," he breathed. Rob heard cussing as he dropped his radio and ran to his mate, his legs burning with effort, and he prayed he would get to her in time.

Please, God, don't take her from me.

CHAPTER TEN

ARIEL WALKED to the main house, grateful that Krista had covered for her this morning. She'd wanted to let Rob calm down before approaching him, and a scene at breakfast wouldn't have been the ideal scenario she'd envisioned, so she'd called Krista to vent instead. Thankfully, she didn't have to ask her sister for immediate help. As soon as Ariel finished bringing her sister up to speed, Krista had insisted on her coming to breakfast at her cabin.

Toby had been sweet, too. He'd stayed and the three of them talked about everything and nothing, family and work. Ariel had been able to get a little better insight into the Woods men—hard working, loyal family who were well off financially, but didn't let that stop them from getting their hands dirty—but she still hadn't gained any more knowledge that'd help point the finger at the reason behind their ability to shift. She'd decided the only way she was going to get answers was if she did some digging in Thomas's office. He obviously wasn't willing to spill what he knew because if he were willing, he'd have told his sons a long time ago. But Ariel didn't believe that Thomas just drifted through this life without seeking some answers. Her latest hypothesis was that Thomas had sought out the truth of his heritage and hadn't liked what he'd discovered. If the news was that bad, why would he share it with his sons?

Ariel figured he wouldn't. But that didn't mean he didn't have proof of it locked away in his personal office, and since Toby had casually mentioned his father's plans to go into town to get some gas and supplies, she knew this would be the best opportunity to see if she could find clues that just might bridge the knowledge gap.

She entered the grand entryway and made a beeline for her destination. The office she'd been using was next door to his, but she hadn't needed to go into it before now. She turned the knob and pushed in, hitting the light as the door swung open.

It was just as dark and rustic as the rest of the house. If it wasn't for the computers, printers, fax machine, and other office paraphernalia, this cabin could be placed anywhere in time.

She walked to his massive oak desk and tried pulling on the drawers. The bottom one was locked, so she tried the middle drawer that was narrow enough to hold pens and small supplies, hoping she'd find a key that'd give her access to the bigger drawer. That one was unlocked.

She pulled it open and rummaged around for a key when she noticed an envelope addressed to her.

From the lab where she'd sent the DNA for analysis. *Fuck.* Why hadn't Thomas given her this letter, and why the hell was it already opened? This couldn't be good.

"Just what the hell do you think you're doing in my father's office?"

Jack's harsh voice caused her head to snap up, eyes landing on his cold ones. "I, err, wanted. Um, I was looking for

Thomas." Shit, she knew she was babbling because she was caught red-handed digging in Thomas's desk. Then she glanced down, actually noticing Jack for the first time. "Why are you naked?" she blurted out.

He slowly reached back and shut the door, the click of the lock so loud it vibrated inside her. Jack stalked toward her. "I was running and smelled you. Do you know how fucking good you smell? It's maddening having you around here. No matter where I go on this property, it's like your scent is a siren, calling to me."

Uh-oh. She stood on shaky legs, staying behind the desk. She didn't know why he had the look of a predator, but she figured it was best to keep the big piece of furniture as a barrier, especially since his penis was erect and so hard it was already leaking pre-cum. "You don't look well, Jack."

"No?" He laughed without any trace of humor, his blue eyes ice, and he continued walked toward her until he was up against the other side of the desk. "I think that's your fault, doc."

"I'm not a doctor."

"Shut the fuck up!" He slammed his hands down on top of the desk so hard it creaked under the pressure. "This is all your fault, you little chemistry whore. I've been taking those damn shots like the obedient little lab rat, and you haven't once thought to come out and check on me. At least lab rats get tended to by their fucking doctors."

Ariel shut her eyes, taking a deep breath to steady her nerves, thinking it better not to correct him again.

"I talked to my dad about this, and he insisted I give Rob alone time with you. Like Rob fucking deserves you more than I do. I told him that the medicine made me feel sick. That I didn't think I needed it to be as strong as it was."

What? Had she totally misunderstood Jack's reaction to the compound? "I thought I just needed to test one of you—"

He cut her off, continuing as if she hadn't said anything. "I came out here to talk to him after breakfast while he was getting his list of supplies ready and I saw that fucking letter you're holding."

Ariel glanced down. She hadn't even had a chance to read it yet.

"When I saw it, dad shoved it in his desk, so I kept my mouth shut. After he left,

I came back in here and read it." He leaned in closer to her. "You fucking little bitch. I know what you've been up to."

Her heart was racing. Jack was all kinds of pissed at her, and she feared if she tried to explain it'd only make things worse. She needed to bide her time and make a run for it as soon as the opportunity presented itself.

"Wow. You're not even going to deny the fact that you had no intention of keeping our secret."

How had he known that she'd considered using them to further her career? She hadn't told anybody about that. And if she were being honest with herself, she had no intention of bringing any harm to Rob's family because that'd mean harm for him. She couldn't live with herself if she'd done that. Truth was, she'd made up her mind a long time ago to never let this secret out, assuming she ever really would have to begin with.

"I sent off samples of saliva for DNA analysis. As a scientist, I need as much information as possible to—"

"Save it!" he roared. "I want the fucking truth." He leapt over the desk and tackled her, caging her beneath him. She started kicking him, but he was too strong. "Admit it!"

"Yes!" she cried out. "I'd thought about using you, but I swear I wouldn't have gone—"

He crushed his mouth to hers, stifling her plea, and she was relieved she'd shut her mouth just in time. He growled when she didn't open up for him. He roared as he moved back. Then he shoved his legs between hers, forcing them open as he spread his own.

Oh God, this couldn't be happening. She looked up at him and screamed for help, hoping someone could hear her. His fangs had descended.

"I'm going to claim you as mine. I'm going to fuck you and bite you, and Rob won't be able to do a damn thing about it because you'll belong to me. Forever."

She screamed again, beating her fists against his chest. She knew this had been a danger when she took this assignment, but God, she didn't want to die. She knew if this happened—if he succeeded in claiming her and turning her into a mountain lion shifter—she'd fight back, and since they didn't love each other, it'd be a fight to the death. *After being raped. Yeah, don't forget about that scary shit.* She had to keep him talking, distracted until someone came for help.

"Why are you so aggressive?"

He threw his head back and roared. "Because your pussy smells like heaven and you're available. It's my nature."

"But—but the drugs."

"Those fucking drugs have kept me from taking you already. They don't change who I am." He smiled and it looked pure evil. "Of course, I haven't taken the drugs the last couple of days. Told you, they made me sick, and since Dad refused to pass that information along, I decided to modify the dosage myself. Figured a few days without them wouldn't hurt."

If she wasn't terrified of being raped and killed, she'd feel ashamed. Ashamed of what she was going to do to this family and ashamed that she hadn't been smart enough to insist on daily checkups with Jack.

"I'm sorry—"

The sound of banging on the door cut her off and she silently thanked the heavens for the cavalry while hoping beyond hope they'd knock down that door and get to her before Jack bit her, turning this nightmare into reality.

"Fuck!" Jack growled down at her, then turned his head toward the door. "Too late. She's mine."

"I'm going to kill you!" Rob shouted, and Ariel felt her pulse quicken. She wasn't sure if it was because she was relieved to hear his voice or for some other reason. It didn't matter. She was happy to hear him regardless.

"Looks like we're out of time, baby," Jack rasped. He reached for her pants and tugged them free just as the office door flew into the room, crashing several feet away from them.

"Get off of her," Rob growled. Toby and Josh were standing on either side of him, all three of them naked. She whimpered, realizing for the first time that she was shaking uncontrollably. Rob glanced at her when she'd made the terrified sound and then focused on Jack again as he crouched down. "I won't tell you again."

When Jack looked down at her and tried lowering himself, she heard a screeching hiss and then was jostled as a lion knocked Jack off her. She scrambled to her feet, grabbing what was left of her pants to protect her modesty as two other lions cornered her, but they were not watching her. They were watching the two other cats fight. She figured Jack had turned once Rob attacked and the others were his brothers, protecting her in case Jack got free from Rob.

She wanted to run, but she was frozen in place, shaking so badly she wondered if she could stay upright if she moved. Some instinct, a vague reminding thought of not running from them prickled and made her lock her knees. If she fled, she could make things even worse.

Oh God, Rob could attack her. Maybe that was also why the brothers stood guard in front of her.

She heard running coming from the hall and watched the mangled doorway as Krista and Mikaela came barreling through.

Krista gasped, and Toby immediately shifted back to his human form. Josh followed.

"Stay back," Josh ordered the other women.

"Screw you!" Krista shifted and ran

over to Toby as he cursed and grabbed her by the scruff to keep her from joining in the fight.

"No, baby!" Toby squatted down in front of Krista, and Ariel just watched as her sister snarled at her mate. He nodded. "I know what it looks like, but you can't." Ariel guessed her sister was speaking to him telepathically, but before Ariel could ask, she saw Mikaela crouch.

"Don't you even think about it, Mikaela... Not in your fucking condition!" Josh roared.

Ariel felt sucker punched. "You're pregnant," she breathed.

Krista, Toby, and Ariel all watched as Mikaela slowly stood upright. "Way to keep a secret."

"I'm sorry, but we don't know what shifting will do to the ba—"

A high-pitched yelped made Josh stop in mid-sentence and all of them turned their attention to the fight still going on in the room.

"You have to help him," Ariel said, not sure where that demand came from.

"If we stop the fight, this could happen

again. Rob has to teach Jack a lesson," Josh said.

"But what if he kills him?" Ariel covered her mouth, feeling sick at the thought of watching one brother kill another. Even if it were to happen because of what had happened to her. Maybe the sick feeling *was* due to the fact it was happening because of her.

"We won't allow that," Toby said.

"Rob is furious, but Jack is still his brother. Now if Jack had succeeded in hurting you..."

Josh didn't have to finish that thought. Ariel knew if Jack had raped her, Toby would rip him from limb to limb.

The fighting morphed from claws scratches and biting to punches as both men shifted simultaneously.

"I think it's safe for her to leave," Josh said, looking at Mikaela.

"C'mon," she mumbled, holding her hand out as she took a few steps closer to Ariel. "Krista will follow us."

"She goes nowhere!" Jack roared, his face a bloody mess. "She's a fucking traitor. She was going to sell us out and she admitted it. Tell them, you sorry-ass whore."

Krista growled furiously just as Toby said, "Watch your fucking mouth. That's my mate's sister you're talking about."

Josh looked at Ariel. "Do you know what he's talking about?"

This wasn't good. It was obvious Jack couldn't stand her—though why he wanted to mate with her, she didn't understand... unless it was just a primal instinct that didn't cater to his own feelings for her at all —but she didn't want the others to hate her too.

"It's a misunderstanding. I sent off some DNA for analysis and he assumed the worst."

Josh frowned at her. "What were you going to do with that information?"

She was a horrible person for even thinking it, but if she were going to make things right, she had to be honest. "I felt it was necessary in the treatment of your ability if I understood as much of it as I could."

"And you were going to use us!" Jack yelled.

"Yes," she screamed back, her defenses all shattered. "I'd briefly considered it when Krista first told me about this. I'm a fucking scientist. It's ingrained in me to re-search the unanswered and announce the discovery to the world." She waved one of her arms around, knowing she look like she'd lost her mind but not really giving a shit at the moment. The fear of her at-tempted rape and subsequent murder still fresh, she was running on nervous energy.

At her confession, Jack shoved a stunned Rob off of him and stood up, facing his brother. "You know what? You can have the lying bitch. Just get her out of my sight."

He stormed out, leaving Ariel alone with the others, the hurt look in Rob's eyes a knife to her soul.

"Um, I found some needles. Looks like he hasn't been taking his medicine," Toby mumbled with what Ariel assumed was a poor attempt at breaking the newly found tension in the room.

"He told me. I should've been watching him more closely. He said they made him sick and your father wouldn't relay that in-formation to me," Ariel responded, but didn't take her eyes off Rob.

"He still shouldn't have stopped the medication," Mikaela said.

Without any emotion, Rob said, "Will you take her and get her cleaned up, Mikaela? Toby, I need you and Krista to make sure she doesn't have any problems leaving the premises."

At the dead tone in his voice and the absolute authority in the command, Ariel felt silent tears streaking down her face. "Robbie," she breathed.

But he walked out anyway.

CHAPTER ELEVEN

"SHE LIED TO ME," Rob growled at Toby. It'd been two weeks since he'd saved Ariel from his brother, and he still couldn't find a way to stop the painful, crushing ache in his heart. He hadn't said two words to Jack since that day. He'd seen him at breakfast, worked as assigned, and glanced at him from time to time during dinner, but as for words, he'd had none. What Jack had tried to do to his mate was unforgivable. As far as Rob was concerned, Jack was dead to him.

He'd lost his mate and his brother.

"We've been over this, bro, and honestly, I'm getting fucking tired of it." Toby bent down to grab a limb in the path and pulled it to the edge out of the way. "It's her job to question the unexplainable. The fact that she didn't go running to her peers with this at any moment she was here should be proof enough that her morals won over."

"She could've asked about the DNA." Yeah, it was a flimsy argument, but Rob still had too much pent up anger to rationalize his thoughts.

Toby sighed. "You're absolutely right. She could have. Just like Dad could've been more helpful and told her what was going on with Jack rather than ignore his own son's health.

All of the brothers were not very happy with their father. Thomas had tried to apologize, and he had seemed sincere, but Rob was too raw to do anything more than just nod at his father when he'd uttered his guilt. He believed his dad didn't fully understand the dangers, but that didn't change the fact that his father's negligence had played a hand in Jack's attack.

When Rob didn't respond, Toby stepped up to him and put his arm on his shoulder. "Look, man. I love you. All I'm saying is give her a chance to explain. You owe her that. Too many things happened that made this snowball out of control. I'm not saying she's not completely innocent in all this, but is it really fair to make her carry all the blame?"

"You have no idea how I feel about what happened that day," Rob said as he yanked his shoulder out from Toby's grasp.

"Because you don't talk about it." Toby crossed his arms and narrowed his eyes.

Shit, he knew that, but it didn't make it easy. "I'm hurt, okay?" And that was the understatement of the century.

Toby relaxed his stance. "I know. You love her." He raised a hand, halting Rob's rebuttal. "Let me finish. I know you love her. I've been there. I know it doesn't go away. You will never be happy without her. That's why you need to talk to her. If not for any other reason than to just give her a chance to explain. She's your mate. I can see it. And as your mate, you need to put aside your pride and hear her out."

Rob squeezed his eyes shut and lifted his head to the sky. He could go see her. He'd continued taking the medication she'd made before she left. Hell, so had Jack. Even though she'd left that day, Ariel had still tweaked the dosage for his brother and had told Krista to get him some Phenergan to take thirty minutes before his daily dose as an added precaution. Thomas watched both of them as they gave themselves the shot after breakfast each morning. Apparently, the modifications Ariel had made and the addition of the nausea medicine had helped him.

"I'd have to get her address from Krista," Rob mumbled, lost in his thoughts.

"You don't have to," Toby said, a little too cheerful. Rob's gaze flew to his.

"What does that mean?"

"She's coming here to bring a large supply of the compound she created. She wasn't going to, but you know what kind of matchmaker Mikaela is. She talked Krista into coaxing her sister to deliver the shipment. It didn't work at first—not until Krista laid on the guilt, suggesting that she should check on the two of you in person to verify your progress."

Ariel was coming home. Rob's heart pounded so hard he felt the blood rushing through his system.

"No," he roared. "I don't want her around Jack!" He'd said that before he'd consciously thought it.

Toby grabbed him. "Chill out, man. Dad insisted on everyone being present for the inspection. I would not allow him to be alone with her. Hell, if my mate said you couldn't be alone with her, then I'd stop you, too. I love you, but Krista comes first. I'm sure that's a lesson you're learning."

"The hard way," Rob muttered.

Toby slapped his back. "C'mon. We need to get you cleaned up. She'll be here in a few hours."

Rob moved woodenly beside Toby, not sure if he was ready to see Ariel. He knew he needed to talk to her eventually, but part of him had put it off because if it didn't go well, he wouldn't have another encounter to look forward to.

This was it.

And Rob was fucking scared things wouldn't work out any better than last time he'd seen Ariel.

———

ARIEL WAS FUCKING scared things wouldn't work out any better than last time she'd seen Rob. The look in his eyes that horrendous day had haunted her dreams and plagued her waking thoughts. She knew it was low of her to even consider outing them. Even if she never went through with it, she never should have considered harming others to further her career. What kind of person did that make her?

No one she could look at in the mirror...that was who.

She'd spent the last two weeks throwing herself into her work, finding the best combination of chemicals that she felt was the most efficient and would allow for time release so ill side effects like Jack had experienced could be avoided altogether. What was more exciting was that because she needed to find a way for Jack to take his medicine without Phenergan and without losing the potency of the original compound, she'd discovered a way to avoid the daily shots completely. She'd researched the natural herbs the necessary chemicals were derived from and had found a way that incorporating those herbs into their diets would create the necessary effect. If her calculations were correct, a none-too-tasty shake every three days would produce the same results as the daily shots. It was the least she could do after sending off their DNA for analysis without expressed permission. And it was in vain anyway. According to Krista, the results had shown no abnormalities, but at least she didn't have to worry about any drug interaction issues due to genetic makeup.

And now Ariel was here at the Woods estate to discuss this new development. When she'd told Krista about it, she'd hoped her sister would be too excited to wait and would just go run and tell everyone else, keeping Ariel from having to make the trip. But no, her sister had insisted on her being here. Ariel wasn't stupid. She knew it wasn't just because she was the scientist and Krista was the attorney, as her sister had so lamely explained. Ariel knew Krista wanted her to confront Rob.

God, just thinking his name made her palms sweat. She'd wanted desperately to talk to him before she'd left here two weeks ago, but he'd been out running in his lion form. Krista had shown pity when she'd told her he wasn't coming back in until Ariel had left. That had hurt her all over again. Not only did she have to face the trauma of an attack, the guilt of neglecting her test subject's needs, and the shame of using them to further her career, but she also had to face the horror of letting down the man she was falling in lo—had feelings for.

You can't even think the word love, *can you?* She sighed as she walked into the main house. Krista had buzzed her in, telling her to come on up rather than meeting her at the gate. The reason Krista had given her for not meeting her at the entrance was because they all wanted to stay in the same room as Jack and Rob once she arrived.

She stayed lost in her thoughts of Rob, life, work, and family as she walked to the den. Josh's little bombshell that day of Mikaela's pregnancy hadn't left her thoughts either. Would Mikaela's ability to shift have an effect on the fetus? Josh had been afraid of her shifting in that moment because she was pregnant. Was it just a precaution or had he actually known something?

When Ariel opened the door and walked into the den, her eyes grew. She knew people were standing around and she could see Jack in her peripheral vision, but it was Rob her eyes had sought. He and

Jack were tied to chairs just like the first day of testing so many weeks ago.

"That's unnecessary. Please remove the bindings." She looked at Thomas. She'd intended on a pleasant greeting and not stating orders as soon as she'd walked in, but seeing Rob tied up like an animal made her go into immediate protective mode.

"I just didn't want there to be any problems." Thomas walked toward her, taking her hands into his. "I owe you an enormous apology. If I'd taken action, the events of that day would have never transpired. I want you to feel completely comfortable in their presence."

"You're not the only one at fault here," she murmured. "And if you want me to feel comfortable, you'll release them."

Thomas gave her a sad nod, then turned to Josh. "Untie them."

Toby assisted, untying Jack while Josh worked on Rob's bindings. Once they were free, Ariel walked toward Jack. She needed to check them both out, but she wanted to start with the easier one first. The fact that he was the more aggressive of the two and had tried to rape her wasn't lost on her when she'd considered him more approachable. She could deal with a little fear. It was the thought of being so close to Rob that she needed a little time to build up her nerves for.

"How are you feeling, Jack? Any more queasiness?" She looked at his skin for signs of discoloration and then looked into his eyes.

"I'm sorry," he whispered, so softly that she almost didn't hear him. Jack had always been the hardest of all the Woods men, but at this moment, he looked so bleak that she had to resist the urge to gather him in her arms. At least she could help him deal with what had happened. She had some other news to share, and she hoped that it would absolve Jack of his guilt.

"Me too," she said back just as softly, then she spoke louder. "You know, after I left here, I had a lot of time to research the chemicals with the medication. Since it was designed to address your aggressive nature, you have to be tapered off of it if you were to ever stop using it. The fact that you were forced to self diagnose your side effects and not take it for a few days caused your previously checked aggression to spike. When I tell you you had no control over how you reacted, please believe that I'm not telling you this just to make you feel better."

"I said horrible things to you. I called you names. There is no excuse for that."

Ariel nodded at him. He had been very hateful toward her, but she couldn't deny the science behind his reaction. "And you apologized. I forgive you. All I can hope is that you'll find the same forgiveness for me one day. Had I been more careful with you, you would not have had to deal with the chemical imbalance that made you more aggressive than normal."

He rose suddenly and pulled her into his arms. Rob shot up as soon as Jack did, but when Jack just held her, Rob did nothing. Ariel assumed it was his protective nature to make sure Jack didn't attack.

Rob needn't have worried.

"You have nothing to be forgiven for. You did the best you could under very strange circumstances. I should never have questioned your need to study our DNA."

"And I never should have let the thought of outing your family secret enter my mind. No matter how the news would have rocked the scientific community, I honestly don't think I could have gone through with it. But it still shames me that I'd ever considered it an option."

Ariel felt arms on her and turned. Krista pulled her into a hug and stood back. "Tell everyone what you told me on the phone."

She looked at Rob before glancing at the others in the room. "Because of what happened to Jack, I wanted to see if I could figure out a way to incorporate natural supplements instead of shots. I've found that herbs derived from the same plants the chemicals are created from can be ingested in their raw form. I've modified the supplement to allow for time release so large quantities during ingestion wouldn't trigger nausea, vomiting, or the like. Based on my results, you can drink a shake every three days and it will be just as effective as the shots while being less jarring on the body. I've brought the ingredients and the recipe."

Thomas's eyes sparkled and he clapped his hands together. "That's wonderful news, Ariel. Just wonderful."

She felt heat bloom her cheeks, so she turned to Mikaela, choosing to continue and not bask in Thomas's praise. "I would never dream of suggesting tests on you while you're pregnant or on the baby once born, but I called some medical doctors to verify that just the herbs in small doses will not harm the fetus or baby while breast-feeding. If you choose to do this on your own, then I'll leave that decision up to you."

Mikaela walked over and hugged Ariel. "Thanks, girl. That makes me feel better. I can't tell you how worried I am about my child having to live a life of solitude like Josh and his brothers." She pulled back and stared at Ariel with watery eyes. "I'd love it if you were to continue researching the effects of the herbs on children."

"I'd be happy to." What she didn't say was that this was something she had already decided to do anyway. Her sister was mated to Toby and she knew it might be an issue one day if they ever decided to have kids.

Rob started toward her and everyone else fell into the background. When he reached her, he stood behind her, rested his hands on her shoulders, and squeezed. "I'd like to have a word with Ariel alone, please," he announced to everyone, and several seconds later, he faced Thomas. "Yes, Dad, I'm okay." Ariel figured Thomas had spoken to him silently, but she was so thrilled this man was touching her, she couldn't be sure she hadn't just tuned Thomas out.

"Are you okay with this, Ariel?" Krista asked her, and turned to her sister. Ariel nodded, unable to find her voice. Rob squeezed her shoulders again and the gesture felt reassuring to her, not that she needed it. Just Rob touching her was enough to get her to do whatever he wanted.

And that thought brought her up short. She moved away from him as gently as she could. She would agree that she had feelings for him, but she couldn't be the mate he needed. She missed him like crazy and felt like he was important to her, but she couldn't lose herself in any relationship. Not again.

"We'll be outside," Thomas said, and turned toward the door.

Rob grabbed her hand and tugged. "That won't be necessary. We'll be in my cabin."

The thought of being alone with him

did things to her body she wasn't ready to analyze. Though it didn't matter at this point.

She had a feeling she'd soon begin to understand just what those things were.

CHAPTER TWELVE

Ariel followed behind Rob, a protest
on her lips that died as soon she gazed at his
backside. Yeah, there was definite attraction. And she missed him. The least she
could hope for was to clear the air with him
and maybe pick things up where they'd left
off—without the guise of testing.

They walked in silence to his cabin,
Rob rubbing soothing circles on the hand
that he'd held as they made their short
journey across the estate. The cabins
weren't far from the main house. Just far
enough to provide the necessary privacy
they afforded those who inhabited them.

Once they arrived at Rob's place, he
pushed the door open and motioned for her
to walk in. As she walked beside him, she

smelled his woodsy scent, could see the traces of sweat on his forehead at his hairline, and lost herself in his beautiful eyes.

"Hi," he breathed, gazing back at her. Time seemed insignificant, as if all that mattered was they were here together. Then he blinked and looked at the door above her head as he closed them in, shutting out the rest of the world. He stepped away, walking into the kitchenette, and Ariel followed him. "I, too, owe you an apology." He turned to face her. "I mean, I still think I was in my right to be angry with you, but I should have given you the opportunity to explain. For that, I'm sorry."

Ariel stepped up to him and gently ran her hand up his arm because she just couldn't bear the thought of not touching him at this moment. "I'm sorry, too. I was wrong and I should have come clean in the beginning. I hope you can forgive me." God, she didn't want to cry. She didn't want to win him over because he felt sorry for her or had a weak spot for women who cried. But she couldn't help the emotion that poured out of her. He wrapped his arms around her.

"I've missed you so much, angel."

She trembled, her body responding to the need that only Rob could satisfy...even if that need was just a comforting embrace.

"I've missed you too, Robbie."

He groaned, nuzzling her hair as he breathed her in. "I want you. I need you."

She reached up and squeezed his arms, trying to find strength to make sure he understood where she was coming from. If she learned one thing from this ordeal it was that she needed to be totally honest with him. She looked up into his eyes and braced herself for what she was about to say.

"I want you too, Robbie, but you have to know that I still don't know if love exists." When he frowned and opened his mouth, she covered it gently with the tips of her fingers. "Shhh, please let me finish. I feel like I've fallen for the illusion once before, and my protective side won't allow me to do it again." She let her fingers trace his lips, relearning the luscious feel of them once again. "But I-I'd be lying if I told you I felt nothing for you. Because I do feel something. I just don't know what it is."

"You can believe it's not love if you want, but I know differently, angel. I know this because I already know I'm in love with you."

She gasped, trying to step away from him, but Rob grabbed her wrist, halting her retreat. She shook her head. "No, don't do this. Don't ruin it before it starts."

He pulled her back to his chest and gently rubbed her back. "It's okay, angel. I'm not going to rush you. I don't have to have a declaration of love or demand that you mate with me before you're ready. I just don't want to lose you. I'll wait for you. As long as it takes for you to be ready."

She pulled back, shocked. "You could be waiting forever, Robbie."

His lips quirked into the sexiest smile she'd ever seen. "I doubt it. But that's a risk I'm not only willing but eager to take." He leaned down, his wet lips burning a path up her neck to her ear. "But that doesn't mean I'm not going to go easy on you. I plan on exerting my dominance over you every time I fuck that sweet pussy of yours."

Ariel moaned. She didn't know if she believed he'd wait for her to feel the same as he did for her, but at this moment, she couldn't deny her body desired him and her soul needed him. She tilted her head, seeking, and he gave her what she wanted. His mouth crushed to hers, releasing a groan that she swallowed and returned in equal force.

Rob bent and lifted her into his arms—his sexy, tanned, hard as steel arms—and carried her to the bed at the other side of the room, not once releasing her from the drugging kiss until he eased her onto the bed before him.

"You are so beautiful. God's gift to me, my angel." Rob removed her clothing, taking his time to kiss and lick every inch he uncovered while he continued to murmur praises as he worshiped her body with his hands and mouth.

"Rob," she breathed. She was already shaking with need before he'd started this wonderful torture, but now she ached for more from him.

"Yes?"

"Please..." She dragged the word out as she undulated beneath him, trying to make contact.

He eased up and then slowly removed his shirt and jeans, followed by his boxer briefs—at a maddeningly slow pace. Once he was in his gloriously naked form, he moved to her again, kissing the hollow behind her ear, tracing his fingers along her collarbone, making her break out in goose bumps.

Ariel grabbed his head, her fingers unable to find purchase in his hair. God, he felt so good. She needed him to stop or she could come just like this. She needed him to focus on her breasts and her clit. The weeks away from him had left her too impatient.

"I want you to make me come."

He chuckled against her neck as he moved south—thank God in heaven—but he stopped short of latching onto her nipple.

She groaned. "You're killing me. Please touch me."

Because if he didn't touch her soon like she needed, she wouldn't be able to stop herself from pushing him onto his back and climbing onto him like a wanton woman.

Hmmm... that idea had merit.

———

ROB COULDN'T TAKE it anymore. His need for Ariel was so raw. He'd wanted to go slow, coax her to her orgasms like he loved, but he couldn't deny his mate. Not when she begged and his lion demanded he tend to the one person in this world who mattered most. He growled as he swooped down and sucked her nipple and half of her breast into his mouth. Sweet Jesus, she tasted like honey. Her body arched off the bed, trying to get closer as she pushed his head down even harder. His little waif was stronger than she appeared. She always found the strength to get what she wanted...not that he had the desire to deny her.

When she started rocking her hips against him, he shoved his leg between hers. He had to let go of her breast so he could grit his teeth at the hot, wet feel of her pussy on him. She was drenched, ready for him.

He had to taste more of her. He kissed and nipped at her skin as he sank lower. When he reached her sweet spot, he pushed her legs open and inhaled, moaning as he licked her gently—gently because if he ate her like he wanted, she'd be screaming with one orgasm after another and be too sore to take him. As much as he liked the thought, no way was he not fucking her tonight. He was going to be balls deep in her well into the morning. He had no doubt. So he took his time, licking her pussy, tasting her essence as she spilled onto his tongue and finger fucked her when she started getting a little restless.

"Come for me, angel. Let me feel it."

Her body went taut when her pussy started to spasm around his fingers. She let out the cry that had his dick so hard it was already leaking on her leg. He thrust, trying to easy the ache, but knew his cock wouldn't be happy getting off anywhere but in her welcoming heat. Rob crawled up her body and took her mouth as he grabbed his dick and rubbed the ruddy head against her slit.

"Oh God, Rob, I've missed you. Missed you so much."

Unable to stop his body's reaction to her confession, so close to the promise land, he pushed inside her, her pussy squeezing him like a vise as he penetrated her fully.

"Fuck, you feel good," he gritted as he took her with long, slow strokes, knowing he wouldn't be able to keep the pace for long. It was evident she had no intentions of him doing that either because she grabbed his ass and forced him to knife into her harder, faster. "Yeah, baby, like that."

She clawed at his back and sank her little teeth into his shoulder as he fucked her like she wanted, like he needed, like they both demanded. His fangs descended and he had the urge to take her. Claim her. Right fucking now.

He roared instead, fighting the urge the complete their mating, and just relished in the feel of her, of her temptation surrounding him. She'd always be his little temptress, pushing his buttons and testing his boundaries. And that was okay too.

More than okay. It would be perfect, because it was perfect for them. What was normal for another couple didn't suit what they needed, but nothing in Rob's life was normal. He had no desire to force Ariel into some relationship because his brothers had followed that path. Rob and Ariel would forge their own. And when she was ready, he'd make her his mate in every sense of the word. Not a moment sooner.

When she screamed his name and clamped her legs around him as her pussy pulsed around his cock, he followed her into that erotic nirvana. He continued to hold her for long moments afterward. Just feeling her light spasms and hot breath on his neck.

Rob lifted his head and looked down at her. Her kiss-swollen lips shook as a small smile formed on her face. She reached up and gently stroked his cheek, and he couldn't help but purr and lean into her comforting touch.

"I feel for you. So much," she whispered, and Rob's insides burned. She didn't have to say the words that society thought was right. He knew exactly what his little waif was declaring.

I love you too, my precious angel. And when she was ready, he'd say the words aloud again.

They had all the time in the world.

EPILOGUE

"WHAT DO you mean you won't take no for an answer? I just fucking told you no!" Jack yelled at his computer screen during his Skype session with Lillian Caldwell. She was nuts if she thought he was letting her work here.

"We've been working together for over a month now, Jackson. I've been giving your company our contractors' information and contacting them on your behalf. You'll just be paying me a salary now."

"We already pay you! We've hired you as a contractor. Once we have everything we need, then you can move on to something else." He took a deep breath, trying to find his fucking patience and realizing said patience must be out enjoying happy hour somewhere. "Your family made a lot of money selling us your land. You have the freedom now to do whatever you want."

"You strong-armed us into selling it! And what the hell else am I going to do out in the middle of nowhere?"

"Bullshit!" *Patience? Where the fuck are you?* "You were going under and we were more than generous with our offer. We didn't have to hire you afterward either. That was my father's brilliant idea."

"I talked to Mikaela Woods and she seems to think something could be worked out on a more permanent basis. She is your family's attorney after all."

Damn Mikaela. If she weren't suffering from morning sickness this morning, he'd give her a piece of his mind. No way would Josh allow him near her anyway. Jack was the black sheep right now. And with good reason. Yeah, things had settled down after Ariel came back and she and Rob seemed to be working things out. Their dad had provided Ariel with a dedicated lab to work in and was putting her on the payroll so she wouldn't have to continue working in Missouri. From what Jack had heard, she'd inquired with some colleges in Texas about getting her Ph.D.

So things were looking up, but Jack would never forgive himself for what he'd tried to do to Ariel. She'd said he wasn't completely in control, but that didn't help his guilt. He was the strong one around here, so the fact that he lost control so quickly didn't set well with him. And even though apologies had been exchanged and everyone ate dinner together, Josh didn't want Mikaela upset about anything, so he kept everyone away from her. Rob was super protective of Ariel since they weren't officially mated, which meant Jack was to stay away from her at all times. It wasn't said, but it was definitely understood. And because of what had happened with her sister, Krista didn't have Jack on any BFF list either, which meant that Toby was always watching him, making sure he wasn't about to board the crazy train again. Yeah, all might be well on the surface around here, but Jack was still treated like a pariah.

"I'll have a talk with Mikaela and my father about this."

"You're putting me off. I know you're just going to ignore me. Again."

How the hell could he ignore her? She had the blondest hair he'd ever seen on a woman. It was almost white and her pale skin belied her years of working outside. Whenever he'd seen her on these conference calls both before and after the purchase of the Caldwell property, he'd always itched to ask how she was able to keep her skin a luminous alabaster. His had been darkened by the sun years ago.

"I'm not putting you off. See?" He reached into his father's desk to pull out a notepad so he could write the message down. Not that he needed to. He just felt like it would get his damn point across that he intended to talk to his family about this mess. He tuned out Lillian's beautiful eyes shooting daggers at him as he rummaged around, opening drawers, but then suddenly, a photo slipped out from a folded piece of paper. He stopped, grazing his fingers over it before picking it up.

It was of his mother. And she looked beautiful, young, and in the prime of her life before her illness took it away. He smiled sadly at the picture, remembering her in this state, which felt like a lifetime ago. She had always been the glue that held his family together and after she'd died, it had taken his father a long time to pick up the pieces and move on. But he'd eventually done so. He hadn't any other choice.

Jack started to place the photo back where he'd found it, opening the old piece of paper to slip it back in. He glanced at the words and froze. It was his mother's handwriting.

He read the first few sentences and felt the blood draining from his face, his fingers going numb. All his life, he'd wanted to understand the reason of his existence. Why he and his family were able to shift into mountain lions. It was something he and his brothers believed would never be understood because his father's parents had died when he was young. They'd just have to live with it as best they could. But the assumption they'd made, the assumption his father hadn't corrected, was wrong. It wasn't his father's doing after all.

It was Mom's.

———

LILLIAN CALDWELL HAS eyes on the hottie with the body, Jack Woods, one of the men who bought her family land and now new boss. She has big plans for Jack, including the getting-him-horizontal variety, and she always gets what she wants. But a night of passion will unlock the secrets surrounded them and change both of their lives forever, in ***Surrounded by Secrets***, the next book in the Woods Family Series.

———

LIKE YOUR HOT alpha men with a side of danger? The Bang Shift Series contains full-length, contemporary romantic suspense novels, featuring mercenaries, mechanics, and the mafia! Start this hot, wild ride with ***Brody***, the first book in the Bang Shift Series. FREE on all retailers!

———

HEY, y'all!

Thank you for reading my book. :) If you enjoyed it, I'd be very grateful for a review. If you didn't like it, then share that, too… as long as your review is honest, that's all that matters.

And ice cream. Ice cream matters, too.
Xoxo,
Mandy

ALSO BY MANDY HARBIN

The Bang Shift Series

Brody

Hunter

Blade

Shelby

Axle

Roc

Tender Tarts Series

Super Hot Supervisor

California Crush

Hardheaded Hubby

Long Distance Lover

Momma's Boy

Part-Time Player

Billionaire Beefcake

Paranormal Romance

Surrounded by Woods

Surrounded by Pleasure

Surrounded by Temptation

Surrounded by Secrets

Young Adult written as M.W. Muse

Goddess Legacy

Goddess Secret

Goddess Sacrifice

Goddess Revenge

Goddess Bared

Goddess Bound

Mandy Harbin is a *USA Today* Bestselling author who loves creating stories that explore the complexities of everyday relationships...with some kissing thrown in. She is a Superstar Award recipient, Reader's Crown and Passionate Plume finalist, and has achieved Night Owl Reviews Top Pick distinction many times. She also writes young adult romance as M.W. Muse because teens like kissing, too.

After graduating college and working many years in technology, she threw caution to the wind and began studying writing at the UALR. Years of trashed manuscripts and rejections eventually led to contracts and representation. With over thirty books published, she now serves on the board of her local writing chapter.

Mandy lives in a small, Arkansas town with her husband and their bossy dog, enjoying her own happily ever after...with some kissing thrown in.

www.mandyharbin.com